Boiling Point

A Charlie Boyle Thriller

LG Thomson

Happy reading!

LG Thomson

ISBN-13: 978-1535181389
ISBN-10: 1535181389

Cover design by Jessica Bell.

Boiling Point is dedicated to
Fiona and Robert Smith-Hald

Chapter 1

The immediate familiarity of the house offended Lenny Friel. Though he'd never set foot in it before as soon as he crossed the threshold he knew it as well as the home in which he'd grown up. The pattern on the wallpaper in the hall was different, but the tired look was the same. The décor, popular for about five minutes three decades before, was a landscape of curling corners, stains and scuffs.

The smell of the place was as depressingly recognisable as the jaded furnishings. The oil in Mrs Macallister's chip pan was long overdue a change. Friel tried not to inhale the lingering odours of last night's meal too deeply as he was directed past the kitchen door and into the living room.

He'd dressed with care for the visit, wanting to impress upon the woman the depth and sincerity of his sympathy, but now he regretted his sartorial choice. His black cashmere coat would suck up the stench of burnt fat like a dry sponge in a dirty puddle.

Friel's regret deepened as he entered the living room to a gas fire pelting out the heat of Hades. Sweat prickled along his hairline and in his armpits. He'd need to change into a fresh shirt as soon as he was free of the dump.

"Can I take your coat, Mr... I'm awfy sorry. I've forgotten your name already. It's the grief..."

"Friel - but please - call me Lenny, Mrs Macallister."

"Okay, son." *Son*. Mrs Macallister had a few years on Friel for sure, but only a few. She certainly wasn't old enough to be his mother. Despite this, she had the air of someone from an older generation. Friel had seen it plenty of times before, the way poverty ground people down. It prematurely aged them, stooping their shoulders, compressing their spines, etching its way into their faces.

She held out her hand as Friel shrugged off his coat. He carefully folded it over before handing it to her. She took it with a nod and shuffled out of the room.

Friel wondered if it would be hung over the ratty collection of jackets he'd glimpsed crowding the hooks in the hall or laid to rest on a bed. Neither option held much appeal, but if it was the bed scenario, he sincerely hoped a candlewick bedspread played no part. Terrible oose. He sighed, resigning himself to a dry cleaning bill either way.

Mrs Macallister returned to the room. "Can I get you a cup of tea?"

Friel had no interest in taking tea with Mrs Macallister, but in a delicate situation such as this his own sensitivities came second.

"That would be lovely." Friel smiled like it mattered.

"Yes," her eyes brightened for moment, "lovely."

He rolled his eyes as she once more shuffled from the room. From the kitchen came the clatter of cupboard doors, the rattle of crockery, the rumble of a kettle coming to the boil. She'd be getting out the good tea-set for him. Silly wee cups with daft wee handles. Saucers with scalloped edges. Not forgetting the chocolate biscuits.

Friel took the opportunity to look around. The room, small to begin with, was crammed to the gunwales. The carpet the kind of swirly-patterned job that could turn you blind if you stared at it too long, but with so much furniture crammed in there was merciful little of it on display. Three-piece suite, display unit, glass cabinet, coffee table, occasional table, footstool, magazine rack and, underneath the window a third table. The drop leaf kind, a hard seat tucked in at either side, and on top a china ornament in the form of a fruit bowl sitting on top of a macramé mat.

Cheap prints of bad paintings hung on the walls alongside a few photographs. Ornaments sat on every flat surface, from mantelpiece to window sills, and not a speck of dust in sight. Maybe she didn't change her oil too often, but it was clear that Mrs Macallister was a dab hand at the dusting.

The room was a visual smorgasbord. With so many knick-knacks, curios and collectibles on which to rest his gaze, Friel was spoilt for choice, but it was the display unit that drew him in.

He squeezed behind the sofa for a closer look. There were more recent photographs of Sammy Macallister framed on the walls, but it was the older pictures that interested Friel. Old pictures, old friends.

Mrs Macallister returned carrying the rattling tray before her.

"Here, let me give you a hand with that."

"No, it's alright, son, I can manage."

She sat the tray on the coffee table. Friel eyed the bone china cups with matching teapot, sugar bowl and milk jug, and the plate containing Penguins and Orange Clubs. Wrapped biscuits - he was getting the full treatment.

"Take the weight off," she said.

Friel came from behind the sofa and sat down while she fussed with the tea and insisted he helped himself to a biscuit.

"I've no appetite myself - the weight's just dropped off since Sammy died."

Friel considered the smell of lingering oil, but said nothing. She placed his tea in front of him before lowering herself into the armchair. Their knees were almost touching but Friel resisted the urge to move, choosing instead to nod sympathetically. To be fair, the woman's face had the gaunt look of sudden weight loss, but her girth was substantial. She must have been a hell of a size before Sammy met his maker.

"Is that Sammy there?" Friel indicated an old photograph in the display cabinet.

"Yes, that's him. Hardly seems like yesterday." She sucked her lips into her mouth and bit down on them.

"He was a good looking lad."

She released her lips, puffing a little at the compliment. "Oh aye, he was that, Mr...? I'm sorry, I..."

"Friel, but call me Lenny."

"Yes... Lenny. Lenny Friel. Aye, the name's familiar

right enough. Now that I think about it, I remember Sammy mentioning you."

She looked him up and down, as if seeing him for the first time. Friel could see her taking in the nice suit, the good shoes.

"Yes, Lenny Friel... He admired you, Mr Friel. Said he could learn a lot from you. You were a business associate of Sammy's, is that right?"

"That's right Mrs Macallister. He was... we were about to go into a venture together before he died. Very sad." Friel shook his head. He could practically feel his heart breaking inside him, it was that sad. He looked her directly in the eye, "That venture would have been the making of him."

She nodded vigorously.

"I knew it. See, I knew he had it in him to come good. If only he hadn't got involved in that terrible business in the Highlands. I don't know what he was doing away up there."

Friel shook his head. "Terrible business indeed, Mrs Macallister. A real shame, smart lad like that."

Ignoring all evidence to the contrary, Friel buttered her up good and proper, laying it on thick and fat about how clever Sammy was. About how he was always talking about treating his mother. That he was going to look after her. Buy her a wee bungalow, and take her on holiday. Make sure she never went short. Mrs Macallister lapped it up good and proper.

So fulsome was Friel's praise, so heartfelt and sincere, that he almost believed it himself. It had been a long time since Lenny Friel had shed a tear, such a long time that he couldn't be sure if he had ever cried about anything in his life, but so taken was he by his eulogy that when tears welled in the bereft mother's eyes, Friel could not resist having a dab at his own.

"I'm sorry I didn't make it to the funeral," he said. "Good turn-out, was it?"

"Oh aye. It was a big crowd. Sammy would have enjoyed it. All the neighbours were there."

"And Sammy's friends – plenty of them no doubt?"

"Oh yes. Lots of friends. He was very popular, my Sammy. He had the gift of being able to make people laugh, but you'll know that yourself."

"Oh aye, he was very funny - a laugh a minute. What about old friends," Friel nodded at the display cabinet again, "like the boy beside him in that photograph. Was he there?"

"That boy?" Mrs Macallister shook her head and tutted. "Him and Sammy were as thick as thieves back then. Couldn't get a sheet of greased baking paper between them. Got up to all sorts, so they did. Funnily enough, come to think of it, Sammy mentioned him a while back…"

Friel leaned forward. "When was that?" he asked.

She frowned, concentrating, wanting to please the nice man in the good suit. "Back in the summer, I think."

Though the day was grey, the weather bleak, in that moment Friel bathed in a ray of golden sunshine.

"Yes," she nodded, "it was definitely the summer. I thought it was funny, because Sammy hadn't mentioned him for years. But no, he didn't come to the funeral. I've not seen that boy in a long time."

Ten minutes later, Friel walked out of the house with his coat draped over his arm. He would inspect it for oose-damage later.

"It's been lovely seeing you, Mr Friel."

"No bother. I wanted to pay my respects."

"Well, you've certainly done that, thanks very much for coming."

She stood on the doorstep of the four-in-a-block, hands clutched in front of her, as if in prayer. Friel placed one of his hands over hers and pressed a fold of notes between her palms.

She glanced at the money and shook her head. "Oh no, Mr Friel, I can't take that."

Friel smiled at her. "It's what Sammy would have wanted."

For one terrifying second, Friel thought she was going to hug him. Instead, she clasped her hands tight to her chest and said, "You're a good man, Mr Friel. A kind man. I can see why Sammy looked up to you."

Friel gave her arm a squeeze. "You take care now."

With that, he turned and walked away.

The black Range Rover was parked just along the street. Friel treated himself to a wee chortle as he walked towards it. An afternoon in Possil wasn't his idea of a good time, but it had been a couple of hours well spent.

Hand on heart, Sammy Macallister had been that much of fool it was a wonder he'd managed to stay alive as long as he had. Friel knew it, half of Glasgow knew it, and in her heart-of-hearts even the clown's mother probably knew it. But Friel had done such a number mythologizing him that Mrs Macallister had bought into the whole package - bells, whistles, ribbons and all. She'd be bragging to the neighbours about her son, the businessman, repeating the rubbish Friel had fed her until she believed it to be the Gospel truth.

The couple of hundred he'd bunged her would lend veracity to her claim. She'd be living high on the hog for the next few weeks. Brand-name vodka, taxi to the bingo, a steak from the butcher's instead of a half-pound of skirting. It was a cheap price to pay for the million-pound information she had unwittingly given him.

Bobby Big Cheeks was sitting behind the wheel yakking on his mobile. He was never off the thing these days. Must have found himself a woman. He finished up quick enough when he spied Friel approaching. Was slipping the phone into his jacket pocket by the time Friel opened the passenger door.

"How'd you get on?"

Friel placed his coat on the back seat and settled himself before answering. Bobby regarded him with soulful eyes set in a big baw-face. It never ceased to amuse Friel that the eyes of a killer could look so puppy-dog soft.

"Grand, Bobby, I got on just grand."

"You got a name?"

"I've got a name for the thieving swine alright."

"You gonna share it?"

Friel smirked, savouring for a moment the knowledge that he was going to get what was rightfully his. And the man who had swindled him out of it? He was going to get what was coming to him and then some.

"The name's Boyle – Charlie Boyle."

Chapter 2

The woman slipped into a flimsy robe before standing up. This sudden display of modesty amused Boyle. As she walked to the door, her pale bare legs flashed in the beam of thin daylight filtering through a gap in the curtains. As Boyle had recently discovered, her skin was milky white all over. Her hands and face as pale as her breasts, her belly. Her inner thighs.

They had been acquainted for a couple of hours. Give or take. That they would end up in bed had been clear from the start. The wonder was that it had taken so long.

Boyle had been drifting like flotsam on the tide of traffic flowing across the country. Didn't much matter to him where he washed up, but as it happened, his latest lift had dropped him in Invergordon, a port town on Scotland's north east coast.

"This do you, mate?"

"Fine."

The driver pulled in beside a Chinese takeaway. Boyle thanked him as he pulled his duffel bag from the back seat of the pick-up. The driver, a diver on his way to a job at Nigg, replied, "No problem, mate."

Small talk had always seemed like a waste of breath to Boyle, but since hitting the road he'd figured out pretty quickly that hitching was a two-way street. What he got out of the deal was a lift. What the people giving him a ride expected in return was either a little light conversation to ease the boredom of the journey, or some heavy-duty chat to distract them from picking over the scabs of their lives.

They regaled him with tales of how it hadn't worked out the way they'd expected. No kidding, bud. They told stories worthy of country and western songs, wailing about the tragedy of ending up with a partner who despised them, kids who thought the world owed them, and through it all they were working in a job they hated to pay off a mortgage that was killing them nearly as bad as the realisation that they were never going to be the thing in life they thought they'd be.

Turned out there were a hell of a lot of disappointed people motoring up and down the highways and byways and Boyle felt like he'd hitched a lift from every single disillusioned one of them.

There were some criminally tedious bastards out there, but as Boyle preferred the warmth and comfort of a car seat, and the feeling that he was going somewhere – anywhere - to standing still in grey drizzle at the side of a road, he quickly became adept at making the kind of noise that made it sound as though he was interested. He developed a stock of key phrases which required minimum input from him whilst giving the impression that he really did give a shit.

Occasionally he hit it lucky, thumbing down a lift from the kind of person who simply didn't like to see another person stuck. There would be a bit of preamble to knock the awkward out of the situation, then the radio would be turned up and driver and hitcher could get on with getting where they were going without talking themselves to death while they were getting there. The latest had been such a lift, radio music still blaring from the tinny sound system as the pick-up roared away leaving Boyle standing on the kerb.

He slung his bag over his shoulder as he looked up and down a street lined with two-storey buildings. There was a pub on the other side of the road. He shrugged and crossed over. He had no plan in mind other than that he wasn't going to spend another night sleeping rough. The local alehouse was as good a place as any to ask about casual work and cheap digs.

It was mid-afternoon when he walked into The Silver Spur. Drowsy time. He took in the WANTED prints, framed and screwed to the wall, the moth-eaten stuffed buffalo head and the yellowing, life-size poster of John Wayne. But mostly he took in the woman standing behind the bar. Blonde hair piled high and sprayed into submission, eyes hard and knowing, she was in full possession of the kind of body a man could happily drown in. The blonde was out of a bottle, but the look in her eyes had been earned over time. Boyle clocked her straight away for the landlady. It was in the way she stood, the vibe she gave out. She was queen of all she surveyed and no mistake.

She was making small talk with a couple of lads who looked like they were taking the hair of a dog that had bit them hard. An old boy with a drinker's nose was sitting by the window, a crumpled carrier bag by his feet, a half and a half on the table in front of him. The only other customer was a wee, thin woman nursing a glass of red wine. Her face had the clamped-in look of a person who had neglected to put in their false teeth. She was wrapped in an old-woman coat, a pair of tatty pink slippers on her feet.

The glasses and brasses in the joint gleamed and his feet didn't stick to the carpet when he walked up to the bar, but all the shine in the world couldn't gloss over the fact that at heart, The Silver Spur was a spit and sawdust joint through and through. Boyle dropped his bag and watched the way the blonde moved as she came over to serve him.

"What can I get you?"

"What have you got?"

She eyed him for a couple of beats. When he didn't crack she rattled off the beers they had on draught. He ordered a pint of Tennent's. She poured it and set it on the counter in front of him.

"Haven't seen you in here before."

"Haven't been in before." He thought he saw the twitch of a smile as he handed over a fiver.

She took the money to the till, brought him his change.

"You planning on coming in again."

"Depends."

"On what?"

"The welcome I get."

"The welcome is always warm in The Silver Spur."

She said it with a straight face. Boyle gave it a moment before laughing. This time her lips definitely twitched. He was still enjoying the glow of a shared moment when the bleary-eyed lads at the other end of the bar called for a refill. When she'd done serving them, the blonde shimmied back on down to Boyle's patch. This time they fell into easy conversation, the sort that flows over the real talk going on underneath.

Turned out the pub had belonged to her dearly departed husband, Hank. Hank had been a fan of Westerns in general, of John Wayne in particular. That much, Boyle had already guessed.

The widow switched the focus to Boyle. Asked him if he was working in the yards at Nigg. Boyle told her he wasn't a rig worker. He was just taking some time out.

"A drifter, huh?"

He glanced at the print of a poncho-clad Clint Eastwood hanging behind the bar. He liked that she didn't ask what he was taking time out from.

"Yeah, I guess I'm a drifter," he grinned.

"Got a name, drifter?"

"Charlie. Charlie Boyle."

"Marilyn. Marilyn Munro."

He raised his eyebrows.

"You heard right," she said, "different spelling."

"Pleased to make your acquaintance, Marilyn Munro."

"Pleased to meet you, Charlie Boyle."

There was a pause as they each eyed the other.

"You hanging around, Charlie?" She glanced at his almost-empty glass.

Boyle didn't particularly want a second pint, but he ordered one all the same.

She poured it then asked him where he was staying. He said he was looking for a place. Asked if she had any suggestions. Didn't bother adding the cheaper, the better.

"There's a bed here as it happens, and a bar job to go with it if you want. I can't pay you much more than minimum, but you'd get your board as well as the bed. Three squares a day. Can't say fairer than that."

"Sounds tempting, but I'm just passing through. I hadn't planned on staying more than a night, maybe two."

"It's not a marriage proposal, Charlie. The job can be as temporary as you want, and you'd be doing me a favour. I'd appreciate that."

Boyle, his head fuzzy from drinking on an empty stomach, imagined a warm double and accepted Marilyn's offer. She treated him to a smile that went all the way through him.

"I'll take you upstairs when Jimbo arrives."

Jimbo turned out to be a short round barman with a shaved head and a pink face. Once he'd got himself busy behind the bar, Marilyn invited Boyle through.

He'd gone easy on the second pint, his mind all about the upstairs. He was bemused to be shown to a small room containing a cold, hard single. He wondered how he could have read the widow so wrong, but if nothing else, it was a place to lay down for that night at least and so he dropped his bag on the bed. He'd slept in worse places.

When he turned around to thank her kindly, she was right there, up close and personal. He could smell the spray in her hair, the talc she'd dusted herself with, the lasting notes of the perfume she used.

"Thanks, Marilyn," he said, his voice low, husky.

"You're welcome, Charlie," she replied, her voice a whisper, her lips inviting.

He didn't know who made the first move, or if it even mattered. The result was the same. His lips mashing against hers, his hands on her body, hers on his, exploring contours, tugging at clothes. A soft thump as he pressed her against the wall. Gasps and moans as she pushed him away, towards the door, guiding him along the narrow corridor to another bedroom. The one where she kept the warm double. Along the way, his jacket was discarded, her shoes kicked off. By the time they landed on the bed, her dress had ridden to her thighs and he was naked from the waist up.

She was wet and ready when he slid his fingers into her.

She quivered and groaned when he crooked them forward, honing in on the holiest-of-holies.

"Do you like that, baby?" Kissing her face, her neck, mumbling into her ear as he hit on her G-spot.

"Charlie, Charlie," her back arching, her hands working at his belt, pulling down his jeans.

Now it was his turn to gasp as she grasped a hold of him.

"Baby, baby," avoiding saying her name in case he got it wrong. He couldn't risk spoiling the moment, couldn't risk her stopping. Not now. Not with this hard-on. He yanked at her knickers.

"Yes, yes," from her as he ripped them off. Both of them groaning as he thrust into her.

There had been no seduction, no making love. From the second Boyle laid eyes on her, he knew that he and she were destined to screw like alley cats.

When the spitting and yowling was over and she'd wrapped herself in the thin, silky robe, she glanced at him before opening the door a crack. She was fifty if she was a day, the years marked by the fine lines around her eyes, the sag of her unfettered breasts. Her sprayed hair was dishevelled, her eye make-up smudged. A smile danced around her lips as she regarded him. She looked exactly like she'd been doing what they'd just done. Boyle grinned back.

She checked the hall was clear before slipping out of the room, presumably to go to the bathroom to get herself cleaned up before round two.

"Marilyn," he mumbled to himself. He repeated the name a few times, to make sure it imprinted it on his memory.

When he was done with the homework, Boyle bunched up the pillows and lay back with his hands behind his head, listening to the sounds of Invergordon High Street filtering through the window as he considered his position.

Pub landlady, warm double, three squares a day.

You've landed on your feet this time, Charlie Boyle.

Chapter 3

It helped that she wasn't a dog. And she wasn't fat. Trailing around the West End of Glasgow after a fat-arsed, dog would kill him. Okay, truth. His heart would keep on beating. Air would be sucked into his lungs and exhaled. But deep inside, in the part of him that defined who he was – the piece of him his mother would have called his soul – something in there would have withered and died.

She was on the right side of skinny. Long legs, nicely toned, topped off with a tight little arse. The running helped there. He admired her for that. Up every morning at the crack of dark, running the streets, working up a sweat. Pony tail swinging in time to her backside. Sometimes she scraped her hair back into a tight, scalp-screaming, bun. That had to hurt. He figured those were the days she woke up feeling dead and so she pulled her hair back until the roots screeched, the pain a reminder that she was alive and never mind the futility of her existence.

She put so little effort into her appearance it was almost as though she was trying to make herself invisible. Pity of it was, she would scrub up well if she tried.

He knew her so well. Knew her habits, her quirks and her tics. He knew stuff about her that she didn't know herself. People gave away so much, and it was all there for the taking. All you had to do was watch.

For example, he knew about her secret chocolate habit. He even knew her preferred brand. Galaxy Minstrels. She bought a bag most days. She kept it in her jacket pocket, surreptitiously slipping the sweets into her mouth one at a time. At least she thought she was being surreptitious. But he saw. He saw everything. He saw how she pressed the hard candy shell of each sweet against the roof of her mouth until it dissolved. He could see how the muscles in her cheeks worked as she sucked at the chocolate, how she almost never crunched or chewed. She wanted the pleasure to last.

In defiance of her chocolate habit she shopped in the local wholefood store. He loitered unnoticed in a doorway on the other side of the street, watching. Nobody paid him any mind. It was dark, the air damp with drizzle. People wanted to get home. They passed by, collars up, heads down, without seeing him. He liked this time of year. Late October suited his purposes.

In denial of the long winter months ahead, people switched the lights on inside, but left blinds and curtains open. Either not realising, or not caring, that their lives were on display. All you had to do was look. Each lamp-lit living-room a theatre stage. Every spot-lit kitchen a soap opera set. It was prime time viewing for the opportunistic. People made it so easy putting everything on show. They practically invited you to help yourself.

But he wasn't interested in petty theft or burglary, not anymore. He had a bigger prize in mind.

He watched his mark through the window. The trendy wholefood shop was all rough-hewn shelves and sourced hessian bags containing foraged mushrooms, artisan breads, and speciality cheeses woven from the milk of free range cloud yaks. The soft lighting emitting a glow attractive to hipsters, students, and the West End literati. The kind of people who congratulated themselves for having the wit to shop there. He felt a little disappointed in her for trying to be one of them. For trying to fit in.

This much he had learned: fitting in was an effort for her.

There was a break in the traffic as she left the shop. He heard the bell trill as she opened the door. She glanced across the street as she stepped onto the pavement. His skin tingled as her eyes seemed to look right into his. His lips quivered. The approach of a smile.

A bus clattered through the scene, clouding the air with diesel fumes, destroying the moment. In the few seconds it took to pass, she was gone. No worries. He stepped out of the doorway and began walking the route he had taken many times over the past days.

A few moments were all it took for him to pick her up. He trailed her like a cast-off shadow. She walked with purpose. Giving off a vibe so obvious it practically had quotation marks around it. It said, *Don't mess with me. I know where I'm going, and I'm not wasting any time getting there.*

She wore the mask convincingly enough to fool most people. Maybe she even fooled herself, but she didn't fool him. He'd caught the nervous glances, the hair touching, the face stroking. The way she stopped herself when she realised what she was doing. Act confident and people will think you are confident. Yeah, keep the act up, baby. You're doing a great job.

She kept the purposeful stride up all the way back to her flat. He hung back as she walked through the small courtyard carpark, watching as she tapped the entry code into the security keypad on the door. He had a fair idea of the number, but did not plan on using it. He had no problem with being direct when the situation called for it, but this was not that kind of a situation.

She lived on the second floor. Living above street level gave people a false sense of security. They thought they were safe from casual stares and prying eyes. Not so. From the other side of the street, with the dark pressing in from the outside, and the lights on within, he could see plenty. He could see her from the shoulders up. Smiling, talking to someone sitting. One of her flatmates. She had two. He could see the posters on the walls, the bookcase, the glow from a laptop, sitting open on a table.

He could see the smile fade from her face as she turned from her flatmate and looked out of the window. It was his turn to smile as a frown clouded her face. He was in the shadows, standing still in the same spot he had been standing night after night. She could not see him, but she could sense his presence.

Still frowning, she drew the curtains against the night. Thinking herself shielded, she stood for a moment, her presence betrayed by her silhouette. Perhaps she was watching through a gap, waiting for him to reveal himself, trying to catch him out.

He waited until she had moved from the window before emerging. His car was parked along the street. He walked to it, still thinking about her. He had to make his move soon, but it had to be the right move.

People liked her, but they couldn't figure her. She was on the edge of her friendship group. He'd seen her in the pub, not getting the joke while her boozed-up pals whooped and screeched like a bunch of oversexed gibbons. She tried. The smile faltering on her face as her eyes went to one or the other of them, seeking a clue. A way into the tribe. But she did not speak the same language. She no more got them than they got her.

Another person, someone less skilled, might think this would make her an easy target. That he would be able to pick her off from the edge of the pack like a hyena snatching a new-born wildebeest. But he knew better. Her gregarious flat-mate – the red-head – would be an easier target. Although outwardly confident and robust, she was altogether a much simpler type. With her, all he would have to do was make a little eye contact and follow it through with a line of sincere patter. Hang onto every word that fell from her lips as though it was a pearl, gaze into her eyes like she was the only woman in the room, and she'd be snagged. This one? Much more complex.

A direct approach would only serve to toughen her defences, and earn him a direct rebuff. She could be got, of that he was sure, but he would to have to come at her at an angle.

All he had to do was pick the right one.

Chapter 4

Boyle held the tumbler up against the light. No smears, no lipstick grease. The smell of last night lingered in the air, curdling his stomach. High notes of sharp cider riding roughshod over remnants of sour whisky breath and lager slops. Behind him, a clack of heels heralded Marilyn's entrance. She wafted in on a cloud of Chanel No 5. What else, right? He turned before she could wrap her arms around him and smear him with her floral scent.

She was dangling a set of keys. She held them up by her face, batting her eyelids, two extra layers of mascara clogging her lashes. Silver charms shaped like shoes, handbags and hearts, jangled from the keys. Fake gemstones glinting in the half-light of the pub. She was done up like an over-iced cupcake.

The thought of all that sugar made him queasy. She'd been feeding him like a fois gras goose since he'd arrived. One tasty morsel after another piped straight down his throat. By the time the signal had gone from his stomach to his brain that he'd had enough it was too late – he was already bloated.

Boyle checked out the numerous photographs of Hank with a wary eye. With a gut that size the man would have dropped off the end of the mortal coil like a lead balloon. The only wonder about his early demise was that his heart had given out before his liver exploded. Boyle had no intention of going the same way.

Marilyn smiled at him the way you'd smile at a dog you were training to do new tricks. *Sit, heel, fetch, beg. Good boy, Charlie, good boy.*

A smear of lipstick had caught on her bared teeth. Boyle's gaze switched from her face to the keys and back again. She was excited about something. He didn't even try to care.

"Guess what we're doing?"

Boyle put the tumbler on a shelf and picked up another, holding it between them. A glass barrier. Plans, she was making plans. The space behind the bar suddenly felt smaller.

"I give up."

"Go on, take a guess."

"I don't like guessing games."

Her throat flushed, the nettle-sting blossom fading before it reached her milky face. She pouted. He was spoiling her fun.

"Charlie, don't be naughty."

She used her sex voice. The one that was supposed to make him fall at her feet, in awe of the holiest of holies on offer between her legs. He smiled at her like the magic hadn't worn off. She smiled back.

"You've got lipstick on your teeth."

She frowned. "Oh, do I?"

She rubbed at her teeth with the tip of her middle finger. Her nail polish the same shade of pink as her lipstick.

"That better?"

He nodded.

She jangled the keys again. "We're going out for the day."

He glanced around. "What about this place?"

"All taken care of."

All taken care of. Yeah, that just about summed it up. He'd pitched up at The Silver Spur like a stray junkyard dog, lean, mean and hungry. Now here he was, less than two weeks later, well on his way to becoming a fat poodle. His body sluggish from too much food. His energy sapped from her continual demands for sex. She was constantly at him. Boyle enjoyed screwing as much as the next person, but the truth was, he was beginning to feel used.

Acting the gentleman, he held the door open for her as they left the pub. Wispy strands of cirrus clouds stretched across the sky, filtering thin October sun. It was the first time they'd left the pub together. The first time he'd seen her in daylight. He watched, curious to see if she would burn up like a vampire, turning to ash before him, but she remained solid and fleshy. No tendrils of smoke arose from her pale skin.

She latched onto his arm for the stroll to her car as if worried that she'd blow away like a feather on the breeze. There was no danger of that. Marilyn was rooted to the earth. Her heels clack, clack, clacked as they crossed the car park. He didn't even know she had a car until now.

There was a chill in the air. Winter was on the way. If he didn't move on soon, come spring it would be too late. She'd have him declawed, castrated, and too fat to care.

He played chauffeur, but she was the one in the driving seat. She wanted to play at being a couple. Go for a run up the coast. Admire the scenery. Stop for a cosy bite to eat. It was make-believe time.

The smell of her filled the car. He could taste her, feel her in his mouth. Hair spray, flowery perfume, and the something else – the otherly scent - that was hers alone. His stomach twisted.

He nodded every now and again as he drove. Grunting occasionally as he wondered why she couldn't see that there was nothing but a great chasm of emptiness between them. He wondered why she had to pretend when the only person she was in danger of fooling was herself.

She wanted him to fill a gap in her life, but how could he fill anything when he himself was nothing but a dark void?

A dull throb started in his left temple when she interrupted her chattering newsfeed to tell him to take the turn-off for Dornoch. She continued her wittering as he drove into the town. She was still talking when he parked in the square and switched off the engine. The decorations from the big golf tournament were still on display.

"Are you okay, Charlie?"

He'd parked on the other side of the square that night with Sammy. He looked over there now. The place where Sammy had lain on the ground and bled was empty. Sammy was gone, but a dark stain remained. Couldn't be, not now. Even if no-one had taken the time to clear it away, there had been more than enough rain. Boyle blinked. *Out, damned spot!* Vague memories of high school, him and Sammy sniggering at the back of the class while Lady Macbeth washed her hands over and over, trying to wash away the blood. When Boyle looked again the stain had gone. Probably just a shadow from a passing cloud.

He had left his hand resting on the gear knob. Marilyn placed hers over it and squeezed. Boyle looked down. Blue veins bulged and writhed beneath her skin. Her rings dug into his bones. He felt the scrape of her manicured nails on his fingers and wondered how much of his DNA she had collected. He slowly raised his head and looked into her face.

Make-up filled the creases around her eyes. In the twilight world of The Silver Spur, she was a bleached-blonde goddess. Exposed in the unforgiving light of day, she looked overdone and unwholesome. They should have been a good match.

"Fine," he replied.

He stretched his lips, trying for a smile but when it felt as though his skin was going to split wide open at the effort, he gave up.

She smiled at him, either not seeing or choosing not to see what was right in front of her.

"Let's find a nice place to eat."

She got out of the car before him. He thought about firing it up and driving away. Pictured himself watching her grow small in the rear view mirror. It wouldn't be the first time he'd done such a thing. He had form for abandoning people in Dornoch and Sammy had meant more to him than Marilyn ever could.

The key was still in the ignition. Boyle reached for it. His thumb twitched, ready to turn. He looked through the windscreen, watching as she teetered along the pavement in her over-high heels. She had one hell of a wiggle on her.

After a moment she stopped and looked back at him. There was a sad kind of expression on her face, like she'd been there before. Like she knew what was going through his head.

He pulled out the key. He was going to end it, and end it soon, but not here. Not like this. She didn't deserve it.

She watched as he got out of the car, a bright smile pasted on her face as she waited for him to catch up. This time Boyle made a real effort to smile back, and when she looped her arm through his he acted like he liked it.

They walked by the boarded-up jewellery shop.

"What an eye-sore. You'd think they'd have done something about it by now. It really lets the rest of the place down."

Boyle saw ghosts in the daylight. Himself and Sammy shattering the window right in front of him. He said nothing. Marilyn continued chirruping. Boyle tuned the words out until she pulled him to a halt in front of a coffee shop. Inside, he declined to eat and ordered a plain, black coffee. The waitress set it down in front of him, calling it an Americano.

They made small talk. That's to say, Marilyn tried to tempt him into tasting the cake she'd ordered and talked about nothing that mattered while Boyle grunted every now and again, just to prove he was still breathing. They could have passed for married.

Back in the car she thanked him for making it such a lovely day. He caressed her cheek before kissing her lightly on the lips. She tasted of butter icing.

"Thanks for asking me," he said.

Bunting fluttered overhead, but whether Marilyn knew it or not, the party was over.

Chapter 5

Jenny Boyle spent her queuing time spotting regulars. The Classic was her free pass out of social hell. Trying to enjoy herself the way her friends enjoyed themselves left her feeling empty inside. It all seemed so pointless. It was an opinion she kept to herself, all part of her effort to fit in. And she did want to fit in, even if it was only around the edges. One foot dipped in the social soup, the other... Well she was still working that out.

And so, whenever she got an invite she couldn't face, she deflected it with a ticket she'd already booked at The Classic - even if she hadn't already booked it. To be on the safe side, she got into the habit of checking the listings every week.

Sorry, there's a Tarantino double bill I can't miss.

I'd love to, but there's a Hitchcock triple and I've got to see Psycho on the big screen.

No can do, it's Bette Davis night.

Funny thing was, as the weeks passed, she really did get into the movies. It got so that she went even when she didn't have to. Instead of being her thing because she needed a thing, the movies actually became her thing. So much so that she got over her initial stress of going by herself and began looking forward to her weekly solo visits.

Hands up, to begin with she did feel like poor wee Jenny-No-Mates. The Classic was hand-holding, arm-enfolding, popcorn-sharing, couples central. Seemed like she was the only person on the planet who ever went to the cinema by herself. But when the lights went down, it was all eyes on Barbara Stanwyck.

Once she got past the embarrassment of being by herself and took the time to look around, Jenny realised that the cinema wasn't filled with couples the way she had first assumed. Sure, there were twosomes, and threesomes and foursomes, but when you scraped away the noise of the communal screen-worshippers it turned out that most people there were flying solo, just like her.

Three weeks in, she started recognising faces. From there it progressed to nods of recognition and the occasional *hi*. Jenny got a warm fuzzy feeling from these small acts of social nicety. They made her feel like she belonged. That in these lonesome, movie-going night owls, she had found her tribe.

Wearing his round, wire-framed glasses, and dressed in his regular saggy jeans and combat jacket, Richard Dreyfuss was a couple of places ahead of her in the queue. Tonight he had pulled his grey hair into a stubby pony tail. Another regular, Goth Girl, was at the popcorn concession. Sometimes she came alone, but tonight her wee flame-haired pal was with her. Jenny turned around a little, swivelling just enough to increase her scope by a few degrees.

The door opened. It wasn't him.

The queue shuffled forward. She bought her ticket then bought a carton of popcorn, more for the excuse of lingering in the foyer than because she particularly wanted it. She asked for it to be layered. Salt, sugar, salt. She carried it through to the auditorium. Half of her in denial that she'd been looking out for him at all, the other half annoyed with herself for feeling disappointed.

She chose an aisle seat near the back. She picked at her popcorn as she waited for the film to start - *Roman Holiday* with Audrey Hepburn and Gregory Peck- and pretended to herself that she wasn't disappointed.

She'd met him the week before when he'd spilled her popcorn, if you could say *met* when you didn't know a person's name. She didn't know anything about him, except that when he'd looked into her eyes, the blistering heat of raw sexual attraction had pulsed through her body. And when his hand brushed against hers, she quivered inside.

She'd never experienced anything like it before. All the way through high school, she'd listened to her friends back home gushing over boys. Fancying this one, being desperately in love with that one. The males of the species were no different. The torrid river of teenage passion had run in every which direction, threatening to engulf anyone who stood in its path. Anyone, with the exception of Jenny. The boys looked like boys to her. Nothing more, nothing less. Not once had she had the slightest desire to touch one or have one touch her. She'd gone on a date before leaving Inverness, just to see what it felt like.

It felt like nothing.

It was no different at university. Everyone but her, it seemed, was obsessed with sex.

In the wee small hours, she'd wondered if there was something wrong with her. If something was missing inside her. She was no more attracted to her own sex than she was to the opposite.

She didn't believe in love. It was just something people said to each other, but it meant nothing. Love was no more than an idea built on shifting sands. And then a stranger bumped into her and suddenly all that mattered was seeing him again.

She'd spent the entire week trying not to think about him. Told herself that she'd have come to the cinema anyway. That it wasn't about him.

Except it was.

Was she in love? Is that what was happening to her? Is that why her breasts felt tight when she thought about him? Why she felt aroused when she pictured his thin lips, his deep blue eyes…. Or thought about his long lean body? It seemed incredible that one chance encounter with a stranger could have such a devastating impact.

A stranger. Yet he'd seemed familiar. Perhaps she'd seen him at the cinema before, but if that was so, surely she would have remembered. The lights dimmed. He was a no-show.

Jenny was still sighing at the bittersweet ending of the film as the lights went up. She felt for Gregory Peck, as he looked back, willing the end to be different even though he knew that it couldn't be. His character's encounter with Audrey Hepburn's Princess Anne had been a moment in time. Nothing more.

She waited for the initial exodus to pass before standing up. Richard Dreyfuss was on the other side of the aisle, three rows in front. He glanced up, caught her eye, gave her a nod. As she returned the gesture, she wondered if he had ever obsessed over someone he barely knew. If it was something normal people did as a matter of course.

She watched his back as he walked down the stairs ahead of her. Another familiar stranger, but one she gave no thought to outside of the confines of The Classic. When she saw him she thought, *there's Richard Dreyfuss*, and until now, had thought no more. She had certainly never fantasised about him. She wouldn't have noticed if he hadn't been there. She supposed he felt the same way about her. Just another loner at the cinema.

Richard Dreyfuss turned right at the bottom of the stairs, then made another right for the exit. Just before he disappeared into the tunnel he glanced up at her. He looked away when he saw her watching him. No nod this time. She'd had her share of nods. Two in one night would be bordering on the over-familiar. She smiled at the thought and felt pleased with herself for not being embarrassed at being caught staring. Not caring felt good.

Jenny took her time walking down the stairs. She felt reluctant to leave, knowing that when she did, the popcorn spiller's face would gradually fade. The fantasy would be over.

She was surprised to see Richard Dreyfuss lingering by the door in the foyer. His face brightened when he saw her. Maybe she was going to be treated to a second nod after all. He stepped forward then hesitated. As he stood there twitching, it occurred to Jenny that he was waiting for her. He was plucking up the courage to approach her. He was going to ask for her number or if she wanted to go for a drink. *Panic stations.*

What to say? How to get out of it without crushing him? Was there another exit – could she make a run for it? Suddenly his face crumpled and he turned away. Perhaps he'd read her mind. No, more likely the horror been clear on her face. Now she felt like a prize bitch.

"Hi."

A touch on her arm halted her thoughts. A voice in her ear sent shivers through her. She turned around and looked into a pair of deep blue eyes.

Chapter 6

When Jenny returned from her regular Sunday morning run, her flat-mate, Andrea, was shuffling around the kitchen in a fluffy pink onesie and oversized slippers. She gave Jenny the once-over.

"You look different."

Jenny looked down at herself, trying to conceal her grin.

"I'm wearing my usual gear."

When she looked up Andrea was peering into her face. "Nah, there's something else. Definitely something – look, you're blushing."

"I'm not blushing – I've been out running."

Andrea's lips twitched. "What have you been up to?"

"Nothing, I'm going for my shower."

"You don't fool me," Andrea yelled at her back.

When Jenny emerged twenty minutes later, Andrea and the third flat-mate, Kaz, were lying in wait, ready to ambush her with coffee and toast.

"You've met someone, haven't you?" Andrea waved a half-eaten croissant.

Jenny poured herself a coffee. "Where's Nick?"

It was a legitimate question - Kaz's boyfriend often stayed over on a Saturday night.

"Badminton," Kaz replied.

"Don't change the subject," Andrea said.

"Is it true?" Kaz asked. "Have you met someone?"

Jenny couldn't stop a grin sliding across her lips. "Yes, I've met someone."

"I knew it, I just knew it," Andrea said. "It was *soooooo* obvious. C'mon, sit down. Tell us everything."

There was no getting out of it. Funny thing was, she kind of did want to sit down and talk about it, otherwise she was likely to explode.

"Right from the start," Kaz said. "Every detail."

So Jenny told them about him bumping into her and spilling her popcorn at The Classic.

"I knew there was more to these late Saturday nights than old movies," Andrea said.

"Shush, let her tell us," Kaz said.

Jenny in the middle of the group, talking, laughing, belonging. Jenny getting the joke. It felt good. Everything felt good. Suddenly all the songs, the films, the books, made sense. She felt like she'd stepped out of a sepia-tinted wasteland into a Technicolour wonderland. It even looked like a movie. Kaz the beautiful blonde, Andrea the vivacious redhead, Jenny the serious brunette - they were straight out of MGM central casting.

"C'mon, tell us the rest," Kaz said.

This is what it feels like to belong...

"Sorry, I didn't mean to startle you."

During the week, Jenny wondered if her memory had played tricks on her. If in the fantasies she'd woven she had enhanced his appearance, made him more than he was. But no, he was exactly as she remembered. Deep blue eyes, a smile curling his thin lips, his body long and lean, and that indefinable something else. He was dressed casually, but he looked put together, switched on.

He touched her lightly on the arm. His hand on the sleeve of her jacket. No flesh on flesh contact but beneath the layers of material her skin tingled. Heat flared deep inside her and threatened to engulf her body. *Pheromones*, she thought, *it must be the pheromones*.

She felt her face flush as he looked into her eyes and spoke.

"This is going to sound crazy – I mean I don't even know your name."

"Jenny – Jenny Boyle." The words doing backflips as they crossed her lips.

"Jenny..." He repeated her name as though tasting it then smiled. "Look, ever since I saw you last week – do you even remember me? I'm the guy who spilled your popcorn?"

Jenny smiled. "I remember."

"Right, good. Okay, that's something. It's like this Jenny, I've been thinking about you all week and I wanted to see you again. Look, if you're married or got a boyfriend or anything I'll back right off. You won't ever see me again – I'm not some crazy stalker, I promise." He held up his hands, surrender style.

Jenny laughed and shook her head.

"Great. Right, good. Do you want to go for a drink?"

"So we went for a drink."

"That is so romantic," Andrea said, "like something out of a film."

"I don't know," Kaz said. "He came out of nowhere, he could be anyone."

"That doesn't make any sense," Jenny said. "Anyone could be anyone."

"Yeah," Andrea nodded. "Jen's right. Nick was a stranger to start with."

"Yeah well, I suppose," Kaz said. "But we were both at uni – we knew some of the same people. He wasn't just a random."

A flash of anger flared briefly inside Jenny as she looked at Kaz. "Michael's not some random."

"What's wrong with random anyway?" Andrea said. "I think it's amazing. When are you seeing him again?"

"Today." Jenny smiled but she was still smarting from Kaz's *random* remark and it felt a little sour inside.

"Be careful, okay?" Kaz said.

Jenny looked at her. The perfect blonde, with her perfect life had arranged her features into the perfect definition of concerned friend.

"Don't worry, I'll be fine."

Chapter 7

"Well?" Friel stared across his desk at Michael Killian.

Michael Killian stared right back at him. Friel expected nothing less. The boy had ice in his veins and he was hungry for it. Friel knew the look. He had seen it reflected in the mirror often enough.

"I'm getting there," Killian said.

"You're not getting there fast enough."

"Some things can't be hurried."

"*Can't be hurried?* What are you doing – taking the fucking scenic route? Or maybe you're just taking the piss?"

Friel eyeballed him. He'd known grown men to break down in the glare of his stare. He had seen the lips of hardened criminals tremble. But not Killian. Twenty-three years old and there wasn't a hint of nerves about him, not so much as a tic of fear or a quiver of self-doubt. Friel narrowed his eyes.

"No, I'm not taking the piss," Killian said.

"What do you think, Bobby – is Michael taking the piss?" Friel glanced at his henchman.

Bobby Big Cheeks leaned off the wall, gave Killian a sneering once over and shook his head. Friel nodded. To say that Bobby harboured no tender feelings for Killian would be understating the case. When Michael's father died, Friel had taken the boy under his wing and he sometimes wondered if Bobby had a case of the green-eye over how close the two of them had become. Bobby certainly wouldn't go out of his way to do Michael any favours, so if he didn't think Michael was taking the piss that would do for Friel.

He sank back in his big black leather swivel chair and tilted his head so that he was staring at Killian along the length of his nose. He couldn't help but warm to the coldness in the boy.

"I want to know where this Boyle is and I want to know now, *comprende?*"

Killian replied with a sharp nod. "I'm seeing the girl again tonight."

"Well, what are you waiting for? Get on with the seeing."

Killian stood up.

"Don't disappoint me," Friel said.

"I won't."

A waft of cold air and noise streamed into the Portakabin as Killian left. The door had barely closed behind him when Friel got to his feet. He went to the window and tilted the blind so that he could look out to the yard without giving much away. He watched Killian getting into his car, a red Audi 5. His movements were efficient. No energy wasted. Killian was a useful tool to have in the box, but too sharp for his own good.

"That boy would cut your throat without thinking about it twice." Friel spoke over his shoulder to Bobby Big Cheeks.

"He'd have to get close enough to try," Bobby replied.

A smile curled Friel's lips but his eyes remained hard. "You know what they say, Bobby – keep your friends close and your enemies closer."

Bobby grunted. "*They* talk a load of shite."

"You boys need to learn to play nice."

Friel watched as Spanish Tony rolled back the yard gate to let Killian out. Hailing from Friel's own home turf of Govan, Spanish Tony was about as Spanish as a slice of square sausage. He had an unfortunate visage, looking like someone had grabbed a hold of his features while they were still forming and scrunched them up tight in the middle of his face. He looked twice as stupid as he actually was and about half as mean, but he was loyal as a butcher's dog.

The Audi 5 drove out. Along with the smart gear he wore, the car was a mark of how far Michael Killian had come – and he had come a long way for sure. Trouble with Michael Killian was that far would never be far enough. As soon as he got to the top of one slag-heap, he'd be looking at the higher stack beside him, figuring the angles, wondering how he could conquer that one as well. And when he did, it still wouldn't be enough. He would always be hungry. Always have that hollow place inside himself that he could never fill. It was a feeling Friel knew and understood well.

As the Audi drove through the gates, Friel's gaze was drawn to the other side of the yard. He watched as the forklift raised a car onto the baler bed. The car, a Mondeo, had been stripped down to its shell. Once it had been loaded the baler lid came down and the hydraulic pistons went to work. In a few seconds the vehicle was reduced to a compressed metal cube, ready for export.

Friel turned away from the window and looked at Bobby.

"Keep an eye on Michael."

Bobby nodded his big baw-face and left. He'd been by Friel's side since they'd been pals playing together in the back court middens, trapping and torturing rats, and copping feels from wee lassies in the back close. Bobby was like a brother to him, but he'd never been one for small talk. Then again, Friel didn't keep him around for his conversational prowess.

He stayed at the window, watching as Bobby drove out of the yard then took his coat from the hanger and folded it carefully over his arm. Though heavy clouds squatted over the city, it wasn't raining yet. Soon it would piss down.

Friel was partial to a bit of rain. The heavier the better. The rain kept the dust down. He liked the way it cleansed the streets, washing away the muck and the mire, diluting stains, carrying away the traces of deeds carried out in the dark. Evidence of wrong-doing swept along the gutter, disappearing down stanks, to be forever lost in the sewers. When the sun finally broke through, it shone on a new world, a clean world, and the circle of death could begin all over again.

He opened the door. Across the yard another car was loaded into the baler and crushed. Killian wouldn't let him down. Bobby was simply extra assurance. Having another set of eyes on a situation had never done Friel any harm. That went for double when it came to this Charlie Boyle situation.

Charlie Boyle. The name was like a skelf embedded in Friel's mind. Inflamed, sore to the touch, in danger of causing infection. Boyle could be anywhere by now. Living life high on the hog, spending the loot – Friel's loot – like all his tomorrows were behind him.

Friel didn't like the feeling that he was being made a fool of. He'd been too soft with Sammy Macallister and had lost face because of it. He wouldn't make that mistake again. Boyle would pay alright, and not just in diamonds.

Friel was after blood.

Chapter 8

Killian watched as Jenny hesitated at the entrance of the bar. The joint was a popular Sunday afternoon hangout, a place where the West End tribes converged. It was buzzing now, full of students and arty types, painfully cool, hip to the extreme, the sound of conversation, laughter and music spilling out onto the pavement, pooling at her feet, making her nervous. She was torn between entering the hive to seek him out and fleeing.

He let her sweat for a moment longer before coming up behind her and touching her on the arm. His signature approach. She turned around, startled, just the way she'd done at The Classic. He watched with interest as relief washed across her face, leaving a smile in its wake. He smiled in return, pleased that she had reacted just as he'd predicted she would.

He glanced through the pub window. "Looks kind of busy," he said. "Will we find somewhere quieter?"

If she'd been a puppy, she would have licked him.

He led her to the place he'd had in mind all along.

Chapter 9

They talked and talked and talked. It was the best – most amazing – time. She didn't have to try with him. There was no de-coding to be done, no laughing when she didn't get it, no having to try to make a fit. There were none of the barriers she had with other people. With Michael, it was all so easy.

She wondered if this was how her mother had once felt about her father, but dismissed the thought before it had finished forming. Enough off that already. Ancient history. Her father had done his best to screw everything up – to screw her up - but despite his best efforts Jenny felt good about herself. She felt alive. It was a wonderful feeling to be part of something, to belong.

At his suggestion, they were drinking *Birra Moretti*. She sipped at the cold lager as they chatted. She told him she had grown up in Inverness.

"Away up in the Highlands?"

"You make it sound like it's on the moon."

"For some of us, maybe it is. Confession time," he leaned towards her, lowering his voice in conspiratorial manner, "to tell you the truth, I've never been further north than Stirling, and I was only there on a school trip to the Castle."

Jenny laughed.

"Are your folks still there?" he asked.

"My mum is. She's a nurse."

"What about your dad?"

She knew the question was coming, thought she'd be able to skate right over it like the mention of her father was no more than a hairline crack, but turned out it was still a chasm. Still a pit of hurt and betrayal.

Jenny picked at the label on her beer bottle with her thumb. Anyone would think she'd be over it by now. Hers was hardly the first family to implode over lies and affairs. When Michael asked about her folks, she should simply have said yes, they still lived in Inverness. Then she could have glided over the pain, the whispers, the looks, the bitterness eating her mother up from the inside out as she ranted that she'd been a fool for trusting him.

"Sorry, did I say something wrong?"

She glanced up at Michael. His eyebrows were raised, crinkling his forehead in a way that made her want to reach out and touch him. The way he looked at her - into her - was exhilarating. It made her feel like she was standing on the edge of something momentous. If she could only let go, anything could happen.

Her mother had finally been able to let go. She danced around the bonfire when she burnt her father's things in the back garden, calling him for everything, laughing as his favourite suits turned to ash. Jenny had watched from behind her bedroom curtains, horrified at the spectacle her mother was making of herself, mortified that the neighbours were peering over their fences, enjoying the show. She blushed even now, just thinking about it. Yes, her mother had let go, but Jenny couldn't. The pain of rejection and the humiliation of abandonment ran too deep.

"Jenny?"

His hand crept across the table to hers. As they touched, she decided that she was not going to keep anything back from him. There would be no secrets.

"The truth is…" *all or nothing, Jenny*, "…the truth is I don't know where my dad is."

There, it was out.

Michael frowned. "That's got to be tough."

"Yeah, well… it's just the way it is."

She said it like it meant nothing, but giving away this detail of her life – that she had no idea where her father was – was a big deal. With the telling she was making herself vulnerable.

She watched for his reaction.

Michael nodded. She could tell by the way he looked at her, that he understood. It was in his eyes, it was in the corners of his mouth, it was in the way his hand squeezed hers. He didn't know the details, the intricacies, the who-did-whats or the he-said-she-saids of it, and maybe he didn't have to. He saw the big picture. He knew she was hurt, that she was all knotted up inside. Well maybe he could help unfankle her.

Be careful, Kaz had said. Be careful of what - letting someone close, letting them in? Other people did it all the time. Why shouldn't she? Jenny stopped picking at the label and let her hand be enfolded within his.

"Don't you have any contact with him at all?" Michael asked.

"He calls me sometimes. I look at the screen and it says *dad calling*, and I don't answer. I just look at it until it stops ringing. Does that make me a bad person?"

Michael shook his head. "No Jenny, you're not bad – you're just hurting inside."

"What about your parents?" she asked.

"My mum still lives in the tenement where I grew up. My old man died a few years ago."

"I'm sorry," she said.

The focus of his gaze moved from her face to an unknown point over her shoulder. The miniscule amount of time this took was long enough for the muscles around his eyes to tighten, for the corners of his lips to take a downward turn.

Jenny's stomach tightened. The familiar knot of unease, of feeling that she'd somehow taken a wrong turn, beginning. Only this time, she felt it more keenly. There was more at stake than her breaking one of the unwritten rules of social etiquette. She wanted it to work between them, was desperate for it to work. She longed to be close- really close – to Michael. They were a fit. She could feel it burning inside her. Michael would make her whole.

"What's wrong?" she asked, her mouth dry, her heart rate increasing.

Michael looked back at her and smiled. "It's nothing really…"

His smile made her feel like she was bathing in sunshine in May, white cherry blossom in full bloom against azure skies. But it wasn't enough, he had to tell her what was wrong. If he did – if he opened up to her - she would know that they were fine. That they stood a chance.

"Please tell me."

As he gazed into her eyes, time stretched between them like strands of warm honey. She wanted to be with him. Wholly, fully, be with him. Their hearts, souls, and bodies entwined.

When he finally spoke, the words emerged slowly, painfully.

"It's hard to talk about… I'm not used to talking about this kind of stuff."

Now it was Jenny's turn to squeeze his hand. "You can tell me."

"I miss him, Jenny. I really miss him. It was like I lost a part of myself when he died. If I saw his name coming up on my phone… I'm sorry Jenny, I don't want to make you feel bad, but I'd do anything to be able to speak to my old man again." He shrugged. "C'mon, let's not dwell on the past… not when the future is looking so good."

When he looked directly into her eyes, the way he did so then, he made her feel like she was the only person in the world who mattered.

Time, which had stretched out so languorously before, played tricks on them, the minutes now speeding by in a blur of conversation, laughter, and the casual touching of fingertips. When Michael checked the time and said he had to go, she hid her disappointment behind a flurry of empty actions, checking her phone, gathering her bag, making a show of not realising it was so late.

"This is crazy," he said. "We haven't even exchanged numbers. I don't want to have to haunt The Classic every time I want to see you."

Pleasure flushed through her. She unlocked her phone, typed his name in contacts and passed it to him to add his number. Electricity danced on her skin as their fingers touched when he passed it back.

"Call me," he said.

She did as he asked, smiling when he answered the phone, saying hello as he looked into her eyes, owning her with his gaze.

"Now I have your number," he said, his gaze making her as giddy and bold as the beers they'd consumed.

"Make sure you use it."

"No worries on that score."

He ordered a taxi before they left the bar and offered to drop her off at her flat. She accepted and sat in the back with him, their hands touching in the space between them.

"Nice place," he said, looking out when the cab pulled up in front of her block.

"Yeah, it's okay," she said.

He leaned over and kissed her lightly on the lips. She wanted to melt into him, to feel his skin against hers, to feel his heat. He pulled away from her, stroked her cheek with his finger, traced the line of her jaw. She understood. Not yet, but soon.

She waved him off, then ran upstairs, hugging herself.

She was in love. Jenny Boyle was actually in love.

Chapter 10

An embryonic smile squirmed in the corners of Killian's mouth as the taxi headed for the city centre. He'd played her like a fiddle.

It had been easier than he'd thought. She'd been skittish as a fawn when he'd been studying her, looking like she'd bolt at the first opportunity. And she would have done too if he'd played it a different way. But he'd been canny. He'd known he had to come at her sideways, but even so - all due respect - the stunt at the cinema had been a stroke of genius. What could be more romantic than a chance encounter with a good-looking stranger?

The way he'd looked into her eyes after accidently bumping into her, holding her gaze, looking at her like nothing else on the planet mattered – he'd been an artist at work. If you could fake sincerity, you could fake anything. But the beauty of it was he hadn't had to fake it, at that moment nothing had mattered more to him than making a connection with her. It had been real.

Beautifully executed though his manoeuvre had been, it was still a gamble. Until he approached her he had no way of knowing if she would be the least bit interested, let alone fall for him, but that only added spice to the situation. Besides, he'd been playing the odds.

Even so, softly, softly was the way to go. He blew into her life like a feather on a breeze, and just as airily blew out again. Now you see him, now you don't. Rule number one - always leave them wanting more.

It had been a long week, Friel riding him, snarling, spit flying, but he'd held his nerve and it had paid off. He'd held Friel at bay and he'd got under Jenny's skin, into her mind. Even better, he knew the password for her phone. He'd watched as she keyed it in, never thinking to shield it from him. Never thinking he was watching that closely, paying that much attention. Her barriers already coming down.

The thing with Michael Killian was, he was always

watching. Watching and waiting, playing the long game.

He took out his phone and composed a text. He read it over twice before sending.

Cant wait 2 c u again x

He looked out of the window at Great Western Road passing by as he waited for her reply. He didn't have to wait long.

Me 2 x

Killian chewed down on a fat grin as he keyed his response.

R u free tom nite?

Any time aftr 7 x

He'd read somewhere that falling in love was like getting a hit of cocaine. Sweet little Jenny Boyle was certainly jacked-up on something. All that dopamine and adrenalin shooting about her system, giving her a rush, making her feel like she was walking ten feet high.

Meet u @ st enochs 730

Great. going 2 call my dad! Wish me luck x

Good luck!

He was getting a buzz on himself. That seed he'd laid with the daddy guilt had taken root a lot quicker than he'd dared hope. He thought it would maybe take a day or so to percolate through, but it looked like he'd be plucking the fruit from that bush sooner than expected.

He called Friel to share the good news.

"You'll know where Boyle is by tomorrow."

He stared out of the window, only half listening as Friel ranted down the phone at him.

Friel was hard, smart, and dangerous, traits Killian admired very much, but though he'd been a formidable man in his day, Friel was losing his grip. He'd lost a lot of face over the fiasco with Sammy Macallister. They said he wasn't the man he used to be. That he was going soft. That he didn't have the stomach for it anymore. Whether any of it was true or not didn't matter. What mattered was that people thought it was true. The sun was setting on Friel's day.

When the rant was over, Killian put his phone away. The sun was about to set on Friel. Killian guessed that somewhere inside him, Friel knew he'd had his day, hence the desperate ranting.

A fully fledged smile flourished on Killian's lips. This was the dawning of a new era.

Chapter 11

"Two pints of Tennent's."

The man rested a meaty fist on the counter, a crumpled tenner poking from his grasp. Boyle nodded to show that he'd heard the order. The man shifted his gaze to the TV mounted on the wall. He didn't seem perturbed by the lack of friendly banter from Boyle's side of the bar. Just as well because Boyle was all out of banter.

Marilyn had been narking him about his lack of enthusiasm.

"You have to put on a show for the punters," she said. "Make them feel welcome. Give them a good time so that they stay and spend more money instead of going home."

At least they've got a home to go to.

He thought about saying it out loud, but didn't. It wasn't worth the hassle.

It wasn't so much the lack of a home that bothered him as the sheer, empty horror that this was it. This was life. Serving pints, servicing the landlady, and making small talk when he could be arsed to feign the interest. He was sleepwalking his way to death. Sure, he could pack his belongings – wouldn't take more than two minutes – and go. But go where? Do what? Wander the earth like Grasshopper? Staying, going, each seemed as pointless as the other.

He snuck a glance at Marilyn as he pulled the first pint. She was at the other end of the bar laughing and joking with Fat Kenny, a regular with peculiarly fleshy earlobes. Kenny spent more time looking at Marilyn's tits than her face, but if she either noticed or cared she wasn't letting on. He guessed she classified the tight tops stretching over her jugs as putting on a show. Like a fly lured into a pitcher plant, it was a show he had fallen for himself.

There was a lot to fall for, knockout tits weren't the only thing Marilyn had going for her. She was warm, earthy, and vivacious. She was everything Stella wasn't.

Ah shit, he'd only gone and set off the S-bomb. He'd made a pact with himself not to talk about Stella Valentine. To not even think about her. He'd been doing a great job. Until now. A vision of Stella arose in his mind's eye, cool and brittle, green eyes glinting, a smile playing on her lips. He put the first pint on the bar, setting it down hard, started pouring the second.

Now he couldn't stop himself wondering where she was, what she was doing, and who she was doing it with. His grip tightened on the glass. A little more pressure and it would implode, shattering in his hand, shards cutting into flesh. If he did it right he would slash the artery in his thumb. Watching his blood fountain over the bar, raining red over punters and pints - that would be something to see. And then, following the spurting of blood would come the pain. The wounds in his hand would gape wide, but the pain would be deep in his gut.

Boyle tightened his grip a little more, if he concentrated, really got into the moment, he might be able to feel the stress in the glass before it gave way. He wanted to feel his skin split, he wanted to feel the slivers slice into him. He needed to feel the pain.

He needed to feel something.

His knuckles were bulging white when his phone rang. Boyle caught his breath, eased off on his grip. He set down the glass, took his phone from his pocket and answered it. Only one person had that number.

"Jenny – are you okay?"

Boyle turned and walked past Marilyn through to the back. The guy he'd been serving called after him – *hey, finish pouring my pint* – Boyle kept on walking.

Relax dad, I'm fine.

"Great – why, what's the- "

A half-laugh from her end of the phone. *I just wanted to speak to you, make sure you were okay…*

Boyle opened the door into the back yard and looked up at the sky. There were no stars, only deep, endless night.

"I'm fine, Jenny."

A pause. So much to say, but how to say it and where to start?

Dad, where are you?

Now it was Boyle's turn for the half-laugh. "I'm in Invergordon, working in a pub. How's university?"

Getting in the question, keeping the conversation going before she decided it was over.

It's okay.

"That's good."

Dad?

"Yes?"

I love you.

Boyle closed his eyes, "I love you too, Jenny."

I'll call you again.

She was gone before he could reply.

"What happened – are you alright?"

Boyle opened his eyes. Marilyn was framed in the door, her face harshly lit by the overhead light, bitten by shadow from below.

"I'm fine."

He could feel his skin bunch up as he smiled, was aware of the muscles working in his face.

"Are you sure?" she asked. "You look a bit... funny."

She glanced at the phone. Boyle slipped it back into his pocket. "I'm fine, seriously. Let's go back inside."

He moved towards her, aiming to stroll on back to the bar like nothing had just happened, but Marilyn stood her ground. She put her hand on his arm, circling it with her fingers, playing the understanding card. She squeezed, pressing the fabric of his sleeve into his skin until he could feel the weft and warp of the material catch the hairs on his arm. The smell of her caught in the back of his throat. He glanced at the rise and fall of her breasts as she breathed, was suddenly aware of his own breathing, of his heart beating, pumping blood through his arteries, carrying oxygen around his body.

"I'm not daft, Charlie – I know you've got a past. But whatever's in it, I don't care."

Sure, he had a past. Didn't they all? Boyle cast a backward glance over his. There were dark places there, demons lurking in the shadows, but there was light too. Hard to believe, but this guy here, this lapdog standing in the back yard grime of a grotty pub in the arse end of nowhere had once had it all. Beautiful wife, adoring daughter, nice house in a nice part of town, and to top it all his was a star that was rising. Him, wee Charlie Boyle from Possil, voted most likely for a ten-to-twenty stretch in the Bar-L, had signed on the dotted line and made Detective Sergeant in record time, followed by a swift boot up the greasy pole to Detective Inspector. It had been starry for a while, and then he had to ruin it. Charlie Boyle had held the world in his grasp and he'd let it go.

No, he hadn't let it go, this hadn't been a slip. This was no accidental tumble. Boyle had smashed his bright, beautiful world on the ground and pissed all over it. It was like he couldn't help himself. You could take the boy out of Possil...

Marilyn pawed at him. He might have been the lapdog, but she was the one begging him to love her.

"You came into my life for a reason, Charlie. We're together for a reason. It was fate - you believe in fate, don't you?"

All she wanted was to be loved. From behind her came the muffled sounds of the bar. Boyle gave her the only answer he could.

"Marilyn, I don't know what I believe."

Before she could say anything else he tilted her chin up and kissed the confusion away from her lips. She responded immediately, her tongue darting between his lips, forcing the taste of artificial peppermint into his mouth.

"Oh for chrissake, get a room will you."

Jimbo loomed behind Marilyn, the sheen of sweat covering his pink face.

"Oops," Marilyn said as Boyle broke the kiss.

She trailed a finger around his face before turning to Jimbo with some words they both laughed at. Boyle stayed in the yard, listening to the shapes their voices made as they returned to the bar. When they were gone, he wiped his mouth on the back of his hand, sloughing smears of lipstick and DNA across his face. On his cheek he could feel furrows from the drag of her touch.

Chapter 12

I love you.

She'd said the words to her father to test how they felt in her mouth. Once upon a time, they had seemed ripe, full of sweetness, a way of expressing a bond she had thought could never be broken. Once upon a time, she had sat on his knee and gazed up at him adoringly, but did she do it because she adored him? Because she loved him unconditionally? Or was it because she had learned that if she looked at him that way he rewarded her with smiles and laughter, and that the reward would be doubled when her mother got out the camera to take happy family photographs that would later – much later - be burned.

Happy families, curling at the edges, turning brown as the flames licked around them.

Her mother called her a daddy's girl. Knowing no better Jenny laughed at the time, she even took a little pride in the label. Now she loathed the phrase.

She licked her lips. There was no sweet sensation, but neither was there bitterness. There was nothing. This was an interesting development. There had been pain for so long, she didn't think there could be anything else. Maybe, without even realising it, she had managed to let go... but she had felt *something*. She pondered this for a while, until finally the answer came to her. Contempt, that's what she felt for her father. She smiled, pleased at having solved the riddle. She lay back, head on her pillow and stared at the ceiling, enjoying the smooth, blank whiteness of it.

Kaz knocked on her door, asking if she'd like a coffee. She called no thanks and thought back to the morning, to that sensation of feeling she belonged, that she finally got it. Of course she didn't, not really. It had felt like being in a movie for the very good reason that it wasn't real. Like the films she watched at The Classic, it was all an illusion, just a game they played.

She didn't mind, not at all. Now that she'd had a taste of being in the warm, gooey centre, she realised that she preferred her natural position on the crumbling edges of the group – part of things, but only just. She was pleased to have learned that about herself. Now it was something she did not have to spend time thinking about. The same could not be said of Michael.

She had already spent a great deal of time thinking about him, and she planned on doing a lot more. The attraction she felt towards him was so deliciously intense it bordered on painful. She ached to be with him, longed for him to touch her. It was as though her feelings which had been lying dormant for all these years had suddenly erupted in one huge explosion of lust, love and longing.

There it was again - the love word. *I love you*, said to her father with no meaning behind it, but oh how the meaning of those words changed in the context of Michael. She had always thought love at first sight a ridiculous concept. And then it happened to her.

She could blister and burn in the intensity of his gaze. The truly amazing thing was that he felt the same way. He had sought her out, taken a chance on rejection. That counted for something. That counted for a lot. And he had opened up to her, made himself vulnerable. When he told her about his dad, it was like being admitted to a private club. He had chosen her and she had accepted. He would appreciate the fact that she had called her father.

I love you. Three empty words tumbling from her lips, but they had meant something to the man who used to sing *Kooks* with her in the car when she was a little kid. She could hear the sad desperation in his voice when she called. She wondered if now that she had made contact he felt unburdened. If he felt forgiven.

Chapter 13

Jenny stared into the dark mouth of the tunnel as the shrieking sound of the approaching train intensified. Her hair was ruffled by a blast of displaced air. It felt warm, tasted grimy. She caught a glimpse of light reflected on curving walls and then it emerged, the carriages screeching to a halt at the platform.

There were plenty of seats to choose from at this time of night. She picked one near the doors with no-one sitting opposite. No eye to catch or foot to trip over. The frenetic beeping warning passengers that the doors were about to close chimed with the pulsing excitement she was trying to contain within herself. It had only been one day since she'd seen him, but it felt so much longer. There was no *only* about it.

A loud hiss and they were moving, gathering speed as the train plunged into the dark subway beneath the city. The high pitched drone filled her head, the rattle of the carriages vibrating through her. She studied the map overhead. Five stops to St. Enoch. Five stops until she saw Michael.

The dark mirrors of the carriage transformed once more into windows as they pulled into Kelvinbridge. Four stops. She checked the time on her phone. She wouldn't be more than a minute late. Her breasts tightened when she pictured his face, the familiar sensation both delicious and frustrating. Perhaps she would feel less frustrated by the end of the night. They pulled into Cowcaddens, two stops to go. Hard to imagine that it was only their second date. She felt that she had known him forever. But what if she'd got it wrong? What if he wasn't there, if he'd changed his mind about her, realised it was a mistake…

She told herself not to be stupid, that he had pursued her, that he was into her every bit as much as she was into him. But the nagging doubt persisted, undermining her confidence, trailing her off the train, following her up the escalator, hounding her until she got to the top and saw him there, waiting for her. And then, *pouff*, the doubt was gone and everything was about him and her and them together.

"You look great," he said after kissing her lightly on the lips.

"So do you."

She caught a hint of citrus, lighter than aftershave. His shower gel perhaps. A tingle ran through her at the thought of him in the shower. Tonight would surely be the night.

He took her by the hand.

"Where are we going?" she asked.

"Wait and see."

They strolled, laughing and talking, everything easy and natural, like it was meant to be. For the first time in her life, Jenny felt like she was starring in her own movie.

"This is it."

They had stopped outside an Italian restaurant in the Merchant City.

"You like?"

Jenny peered through smoky windows into a warm room glowing with candlelight.

"I like," she said.

The waiter greeted Michael by name and led them to a booth.

"He knows your name," she whispered when he'd gone. "You must come here a lot."

Michael smiled. "It's my regular place... I live just around the corner."

He did that thing he did, gazing right into her eyes, right inside her, and Jenny did that thing she did in response. She quivered inside.

The evening went by in a whirl of talk, laughter and food. There were pauses in their conversation, but none were the uncomfortable kind. Just a little time out for gazing into each other's eyes and the light caressing of fingers reaching towards each other on the table. Michael's hands were narrow, his fingers long and strong, nails neatly trimmed and clean.

The waiter cleared the plates from their table and asked if they would like to see the dessert menu. Michael checked his watch.

"No thanks, just the bill when you're ready."

The waiter nodded. *This is it,* Jenny thought, *this is when he asks me back to his place.* Michael put his hand over hers, his skin cool to the touch. She wondered how he always seemed so cool, and if he ever broke out in a sweat. She would find out soon enough. The thought making her smile on the outside while she felt warm and gooey inside.

"I'm sorry," he said, "I've got an early start – I'll have to call it a night."

Her smile faltered. The bill appeared, Michael paid in cash, not allowing any suggestion that she should contribute.

"My treat, okay? I insist." He asked the waiter to order a taxi.

Michael was at her elbow as she stood up, carrying her bag, steering her through the tables to the door. The waiter had their jackets waiting for them, then they were out of the warmth into the cold, the taxi already sitting at the kerb. Michael opened the door and gave the driver Jenny's address.

"I'll call you, okay?"

A quick peck on the cheek and she was in the back seat, her bag on her lap. The taxi pulling away from the kerb before she had finished buckling her seatbelt. She turned to look out of the back window, her hand ready to wave, but the street was empty.

Jenny turned round and stared straight ahead, wondering what the hell had just happened. The night she thought was going to be *the* night had ended with a perfunctory kiss. It was as if a switch had gone off inside him. Warm to cold, just like that.

No, not cold, more brusque and business like. But what kind of business? An early start, he'd said, but an early start for what? Funny the things she knew about him and the things she didn't... She knew that his favourite film was *La*

Dolce Vita, his favourite book *Brave New World*, and that he regretted not being on speaking terms with his father when he died. She knew he lived somewhere in or around the Merchant City, but not where exactly, not even the street. His clothes and attitude hinted at him being well paid, but she did not know how he earned his money. So many little details – like his love of Miles Davis – so many big gaps.

The taxi pulled up in front of her block. "This okay for you?" the driver asked.

"Fine, thanks. How much do I owe you?" She opened her bag to look for her purse.

"Already paid," the driver said.

She looked up and saw him staring at her in the rear view mirror.

"Okay, thanks," she said.

"Wasn't me that paid it," he said.

Creep. She fumbled at the door handle, experiencing a brief moment of panic when she thought the driver had locked her in the taxi, then it opened and she was out on the street. The taxi didn't linger. She stared after its red tail lights, before walking to the entrance to her block. Her legs felt heavy as she climbed the stairs. She hoped, hoped, hoped Kaz and Andrea weren't around. They'd know as soon as they looked at her that something was up. She wasn't in the mood for a post mortem of her evening and she didn't have the energy for a cover-up.

The communal areas of the flat were empty. Her flat-mates may have been in their rooms, but Jenny didn't hang around to find out. She went straight to her own room and locked the door behind her. She took off her jacket, threw it over the chair, kicked off her boots and flopped on the bed.

She stared at the ceiling arguing it out with herself. There was no reason for her to feel so deflated, the whole *this is the night* thing had been in her head, Michael hadn't suggested it. All he'd done was say he had to have an early night, so why did she feel so deflated?

It was her own fault – she shouldn't have built the whole thing up in her head so much. He'd said he would call her and she had no reason to think he wouldn't… but still she couldn't let it go – the way he had switched – they'd gone from having a romantic evening to him hustling her out of the restaurant at top speed.

She'd got it wrong, made a complete fool of herself. She'd been better as she was – on the periphery, kind-of-friends with everyone, special friends with no-one, accepted as being a little bit odd, but accepted nevertheless. She should have carried on being a loner instead of getting carried away with herself. She was a fool, had been a fool, and it hurt.

If she was wrong about Michael, then what else was she wrong about? Had she ever been right about anything? Every decision based on a false premise, her ideas built on a foundation of shifting sand.

Michael had knocked on the door and she had let him in, but she didn't know who she was letting in. She'd cast him in the role of leading man, his Bogart to her Bacall, but maybe she'd let in the Bogey Man instead. All these years of protecting herself, keeping her feelings wrapped up tight, and now she was so unravelled she didn't know who she was anymore.

Jenny lay on the bed staring silently at the ceiling, but inside she was screaming. If she didn't do something soon she would go insane or explode. In the morning they would find the walls streaked with her blood, her guts hanging from the ceiling, and on the bed, lying in the broken cradle of her rib cage, they would find the black, shrivelled husk that had once been her heart.

Enough.

She needed to do something. She should text him, thank him for the meal. She sat up, wondering why she hadn't thought of it before, trying to ignore the voice in her head telling her that it was because she didn't want him to think she was stalking him, or that she was the obsessive, possessive type.

She picked up her bag. One simple text was hardly bunny boiling territory. She opened the bag and felt inside for her phone. On not finding it, she opened it wider and peered inside. It was usually lying near the top, easily accessed. She gave the bag a shoogle. No phone. She frowned, and had a rummage, then a more serious rummage. When she still couldn't find it she dumped the contents of the bag on her bed. She could see immediately that her phone wasn't there, but as she did not believe what her eyes were telling her, she rooted through her things – notepad, purse, lip salve, tissues, pens, scrunchies, empty Minstrel packet, and definitely no phone.

She got up off the bed and checked the pockets of her jacket, then she checked them again with the same result – no phone.

Jenny looked around the room as though the answer was right there in front of her and if only she looked hard enough she would see it, but it turned out that no matter how hard she looked the answer was still the same – no phone.

Lost, stolen or simply misplaced, it all came down to the same thing – she had no way of contacting Michael.

Chapter 14

Boyle pushed the glass against the optic for a second, then a third time before adding a dash of tonic. Long on G, short on T was how he liked his end of shift drink. He held the glass up to the light, appreciating for a moment the oily swirl of gin through tonic.

He shuddered as the first bitter mouthful went down. The botanicals came through on the second taste, the buzz came on with the third, the warm glow radiating from his mouth, hitting his brain, taking the edge off.

It was at this precise point in the day, with the gin kicking in, pub closed, Marilyn out of eye, ear and mouth - *freshening up* – that Boyle got within shouting distance of being at ease with the world and his place in it. He knew it was an illusion, as impossible to hold on to as the buzz from the first drink. He'd have another, trying to maintain the kick, but it was never the same. But he'd keep trying, oh yes, he'd keep on trying, because if he was anything he was a trier. He'd try and try and try again, like Robert the fucking Bruce.

Boyle put so much effort into holding onto the buzz that he woke up every morning coated in a sweaty slick of self-loathing with the thick taste of deadened juniper in his mouth. But it didn't stop him trying.

He thought about calling Jenny. He'd been thinking about it off and on since she'd called him. He took his phone from his pocket and stared at the dark screen. His reflection stared back at him, his face as desolate a landscape as his past. The lines ran deep, every relationship either broken or getting there. Not for the first time, it occurred to Boyle that the only good thing to come out of his life was his daughter. Funny to think a child so pure and sweet could come from him.

You're too hard on yourself, Charlie. You're not all bad. In fact, you're not a bad lad. Phone the girl. Phone your daughter. Tell her you love her. Tell her you're sorry for tearing her world apart, for turning her sweet mother into a bitter shrew, for not being there for either of them. For being a shit husband and a lousy father. Pick up the phone, Charlie, and tell her you're sorry.

He looked away from the screen. No good ever came from delving into the past, especially not when the delving was aided by a bottle of gin. The truth was, what frightened him most when he did go there was how few regrets he really had. He was sorry for how things were between him and Jenny but a couple of inches into the bottle the darkest recesses of his heart revealed enough of their secrets for him to know that he would do the same things over again – only this time he'd work it so that he got what he wanted.

Jenny had been the one who rejected him, she had been the one who turned her head in the street when she saw him. She was the one who refused his calls but the truth was, she was better off without him.

He swallowed the last mouthful in the glass, wondering if he'd have time for another quiet one before Marilyn clacked back in, skirt tight, heels high, pulse points freshly drenched in perfume, trying to cover up the smell of desperation. A wave of disgust at himself rolled in with the thought. He couldn't keep on blaming her for not being Stella.

There it was again – the S-word. *Get thee behind me, Stella.* He laughed to himself. Maybe he would have that second drink. And maybe it wouldn't kill him to be nice to Marilyn. Yeah, he'd play nice and let her be nice to him.

He was about to make a return trip to the optic when his phone lit up. *Jenny!* As if to prove he still had one, Boyle's heart gave a little rat-a-tat-tat. He answered the call with the smile on his face riding his voice. Forget the past, maybe it was time to make a future.

"Jenny?"

Hello Charlie.

A male voice. Boyle frowned. "Who is this? Where's Jenny?"

Relax Charlie – your lassie's fine… at least she is for now…

Glasgow accent, grit in the throat.

"What do you mean – what have you done to her?"

Boyle's fingers curled into a fist. "I swear, if you've- "

I told you already, Charlie – she's fine – and if you want her to stay that way you'd better get back in your box.

Boyle sucked in a deep breath and closed his eyes. "What do you want?" he asked, the words coming out screwed up tight as his fist.

I want what's owed me.

"Owed? I don't know what you're talking-"

No? Did Sammy never mention me? My feelings are hurt. Here, let me help you. The name's Friel. Lenny Friel.

The name came wheeling out of the past like a juggernaut. Sammy had mentioned Friel. He'd been showing off, letting Boyle know that he was out playing with the big boys.

"The name's familiar now that you mention it, but Sammy's dead."

Appreciate the update, Charlie. I am aware that Sammy is with the angels - God rest his soul - but his debt is alive and kicking.

"What debt?" Boyle didn't much fancy where this was leading.

I'm talking about the money your pal owed me. He liked the gee-gees, Sammy. Did you know that? Liked them a bit too much, if you get my drift. And then there was the coke habit he developed. Expensive business. That job was supposed to clear what he owed but Sammy met his maker before he squared up and now I want paying – with interest.

Boyle's skin goose-fleshed as a multitude of thoughts careened around his head. "I don't have-"

Take a minute to think about what you're going to say next, Charlie, and see when you've taken that minute? Make sure it's something I want to hear… Nice looking lassie, your daughter, be good if she stayed that way.

"If you touch her I'll-"

Are you threatening me, Charlie?

Boyle's mind whirled. "No. You'll get paid, but I need time."

Clock's ticking, Charlie. Tick tock.

"But where – when –"

I'll let you know.

The line went dead. Boyle lowered the phone, his mind racing, running through question after question, his fist clenching and unclenching, his lips drawn tight against his teeth. *Jesus fuck Sammy, what have you got me into?* Then suddenly, a prickling on his neck. He turned. Marilyn standing at the other end of the bar, all lipsticked up and no place to go. He was breathing in perfume, only just catching on to the fact that he'd been breathing it in for some time.

"How long have you been there?" His voice a rasp.

"Long enough. Past catching up with you, Charlie?"

"Something like that."

"You leaving?"

"I'm leaving," he said.

"Got time for a drink before you go?"

Boyle looked at the empty glass and back at Marilyn. She deserved better. He wished he could put more feeling into the thought.

"Better forget about the drink."

She looked away, staring into nothing, as he brushed by.

Upstairs, he took his duffel bag from the bottom of the wardrobe and packed his gear. It didn't take long. Before going back down, he took off the shirt he was wearing - one Marilyn had bought for him — and changed into the long-sleeve charcoal top he'd been wearing when he arrived.

She was at the bottom of the stairs waiting for him. He walked down, visions of crying and wailing, of a screaming, mascara-streaked face dancing in his head, but her face was fixed, composed in chin-up-don't-let-the-bastards-grind-you-down defiance. *Good on you, girl.* He felt proud of her, though he knew he had no right. No matter, some other guy would blow in. She wasn't the type to be lonely for long. He reached the bottom step.

"This'll be goodbye then," she said.

"It's been nice knowing you," he replied.

"Wish I could say the same. "

"Don't be like that, Marilyn — I never made you any

promises."

"No… no, you didn't."

She turned her face away from him. He cupped her cheek with his hand and when she didn't pull away he turned her face back towards his and kissed her on the lips, long and sweet for goodbye.

"You take care," he said.

"Yeah, Charlie, you too."

Boyle was on his way through the door when he felt her hand on his arm.

"Ah, Marilyn, honey – I've gotta go –"

"No – that's not it."

He turned to her. "Here, take this." She took his hand and pressed something into his palm.

Boyle looked and shook his head, "Marilyn, I can't."

"I want you to – really."

"You sure?"

"Take it."

"I'll bring it back, I promise."

"Don't start making promises, Charlie – not now."

He smiled, "Thanks, Marilyn."

Boyle walked out of the front door of The Silver Spur without looking back. He wiped his mouth on the back of his hand as he crossed the carpark, the rattling echo of the bolts being pushed home fading behind him. He unlocked the car with the key she had pressed on him, not that he'd taken much persuasion. The car was going to get him where he needed to be a lot sooner than he'd have otherwise managed. Problem was, he wasn't entirely sure where he needed to get.

By the time he was in the driver's seat, all thoughts of Marilyn and The Silver Spur had gone from his mind. Every thought, every thread, led him to the same place.

Stella – Boyle had to find Stella.

Chapter 15

Killian snapped awake three seconds before his alarm sounded. His morning routine began with the emptying of his bladder followed by his morning workout. He exercised in the moment, his mind entirely focused on his body. Every muscle, every sinew, stretched and worked, breathing regulated, each movement deliberate, controlled, intense. Nothing wasted. By the end of the routine his body, naked save for a pair of trunks, was slick with sweat.

He studied himself in the full-length mirror, a critical assessment with a cool eye. His body was streamlined, carrying no excess fat, flab, chub or muscle. He was streamlined, not musclebound, fit, effective, in control. His shower was brisk, his shave precise. When his toilette was over he spent some time practicing his expressions.

Only once he was dressed, his bed made, and coffee poured did Killian allow himself to consider the events of the night before. Friel's pleasure in snaring Boyle had been evident in the rattlesnake gleam of his eyes. Boyle would cough up the diamonds, Macallister's debt would be paid, and – hire a band, put out the flags - Friel's face would be saved, his position at the top of the heap assured.

Friel had sat back in his big, fat leather chair, shirt buttons straining on a thickening torso, a smile snaking across his lips and said, "Good call using the daughter."

Killian nodded, picturing himself smashing Friel's skull in with a hammer. He wondered if it would be possible to strike fast enough and hard enough so that Friel died with the smile still on his face.

"How's that working out for you?" Friel asked.

"Sweet," Killian said.

"Good. I like to see a man happy in his work."

Friel laughed. Killian laughed along with him, picturing the gunk from Friel's mashed up brain dripping from the desk, his grey matter splattering the filing cabinet as his blood clotted on the floor. The double-barrelled laughter rang cold and didn't last for long.

"Just remember, Michael, I'm looking for subtlety here. No alarms going off – she can't just disappear, understand?"

Killian nodded, "Understood."

"I don't want any ripples, nothing that's going to draw attention to Boyle. The only eyes I want on that bastard are mine."

Killian shivered in the damp air as he left Friel's office. *Now that we've got the hook into Boyle we've got to keep the pressure on.* The yard was all sharp edges and deep shadows, the machines lying dormant. *You know what to do.* Yeah, Killian knew what to do alright. Spanish Tony let him out, closing the gates to Friel's kingdom behind him.

Friel had built the salvage and wrecking business up from scratch, using it as a legit cover for his more lucrative and less lawful streams of income. He was a ruthless operator, managing to maintain his top dog, A-Number One, head honcho status for a couple of decades, slapping down all contenders, disappearing a few of them along the way. The car baler had come in handy on more than one occasion. Bones, blood and internal organs compressed in a metal cube and exported to China, India, Taiwan. But nobody in this business survived for long on yesterday's reputation. The Sammy Macallister situation had done Friel no favours. Killian had picked up on the rumours - word was Friel was losing the edge, he'd had his day, was going as soft as soap.

There was truth in it for sure, Friel had made a bad call, had let Sammy take the piss with his coke and gambling debts, but Friel wasn't ready for leathering his skin on the Costa del Sol just yet. The way Killian figured it, not only was Friel desperate to save face, he'd want to make a big show of the saving.

All well and good. Let Friel carry on with salvaging what was left of his rep. Killian would bide his time. He was in it for the long game. He'd play it smart, let yesterday's top dog have his day, then snap his neck when he was least expecting it.

In some ways slaughtering Friel would be more like killing his father than killing his actual father.

Killian started making his own money when he was nine years old by selling single fags and shop-lifted confectionary to schoolmates. By the time he was thirteen he'd graduated to dealing drugs and alcohol. It was when he attempted to expand his narcotics business by moving in to new territories – that is, different schools – and undercutting the prices of the regular dealers in escapism that he unwittingly brought himself to the attention of Lenny Friel. Friel did not look kindly upon interlopers. No-one who knew him would have been surprised if the boy had been found face down in the Forth and Clyde, but instead of squashing him like a fly, Friel took the young Michael Killian under his wing.

From the start, Killian was in thrall to Friel, recognising him as someone he could learn from, and learn he did. By the age of sixteen, Killian was making more money than most of his teachers, supplementing his income by supplying a handful of them with hash. He never sampled the product himself – taking drugs was a game for mugs. When the same teachers told Killian he was smart enough to go to university he laughed in their faces and told them to fuck off.

Back then he would have taken a hit for Friel, and sacrificed himself willingly, but the sun had long since set on those days.

Killian finished his coffee and loaded his Nutribullet with kale, melon, banana, apple and a few walnuts. Maybe he'd mix one up for Friel. Load it with malt whisky, a couple of cigars, an artery-choking fry up, and top it off with a big, greasy cholesterol-laden fish supper.

He smiled at the thought. Friel would sooner pluck out the jelly of his own eye than eat a slice of wholemeal bread. He was old school all the way back to the Cretaceous period. He had looked at the young Michael Killian and seen himself reflected back, but his eyes had played tricks on him. Killian was a new breed - leaner, meaner, sharper. He blitzed his breakfast thinking Darwin had got it right.

Survival of the fittest.

It was still dark when he got into his car and drove out to the West End. He parked along the street from Jenny's flat and waited. Eight minutes later she ran towards him.

Chapter 16

Knock, knock, knock, knock, knock, knock, knock.

Boyle woke with a stiff neck, a gummy mouth and an urge to kill the bastard who was rapping on the top of his head. He squinted his eyes open. He was looking up the nostrils of a man who could have passed for Mr Potato Head if he'd had a moustache.

Mr P had his knuckles primed for another knock on the car window. Funny, felt like he'd been banging right on Boyle's skull. Boyle flapped his hand, *cut it out.* He swore to himself, if the guy rapped one more time Boyle would punch him on the nose. Lucky for Mr P, he held his rap in reserve as Boyle fumbled to get his seat upright.

"Are you alright in there?" Mr P, his big mouth spitting through the ventilation crack Boyle had left at the top of the window.

"Yeah, yeah," he replied. "Gimme a minute."

Seat sorted, he opened the door. Mr P filling the gap as soon as it appeared. He had a wee dog on a lead. It was all wire hair and excitement as it tried to scramble into the car.

"Settle down Bernice," he told the dog, and said to Boyle, "Are you alright?"

Bernice? Boyle scratched the dog's ears.

"Yeah, fine."

"Oh… good – it's just that I saw you slumped in the car…"

Boyle pushed the door wider revealing Mr P in his full glory - beige slacks, russet brogues, chocolate blouson jacket.

"Brown," Boyle said, getting out of the car. His head still thick from bad sleep. To think, only a few weeks before he'd reckoned on waking up to the sound of pounding surf, blue skies above his head, warm sand beneath his feet.

"Sorry?" Mr P took a step back. He looked like he was regretting poking this particular bear with a stick.

"You favour a brown palette," Boyle said.

Mr P looked down at his clothes. "Oh, yes – I see. And

you… you favour black."

"Yup." Boyle twisted his neck, trying to break the crick. "Been travelling overnight," he said. "Got here too early to go knocking on doors, so I thought I'd grab a few zeds."

"Whose door were you thinking about knocking on… if you don't mind me asking?"

"It's a sad tale, friend. Do you live in the neighbourhood?"

Mr P nodded enthusiastically. There was a stranger in town, and he was getting first dibs on the goss. "Yes, just down the street."

Bingo. Boyle had struck information gold. If anyone could give him the gen on Stella's whereabouts, it would be the Daily Bugle here. Boyle had come across the type plenty of times when he'd been on the job. Generally retired or semi-retired, upstanding members of the community all, male or female, they made it their business to know everybody's business.

"Then you'll know about the passing of Frank Valentine?" Boyle said.

Mr P tutted and shook his head. "Bad business, very sad…"

Boyle mirrored the head shaking and put on his Eeyore face as he spun his yarn. "It is that… I only just heard the news myself – I'm an old friend of Frank's. I wanted to pay my respects to Mrs Valentine-"

"Now that's a shame, a real shame – Mrs Valentine isn't here at the moment. I hope you haven't had a completely wasted journey Mr…?"

"Grant," Boyle said. "John Grant." He proffered his hand.

"Dench," Mr P shook Boyle's hand, "Bruce Dench. Pleased to meet you."

"Likewise. Mrs Valentine isn't here you say?"

Boyle very well knew Stella wasn't at home. Had discovered the fact for himself in the wee small hours when Mr Dench was tucked up beside Mrs Dench, Bernice snoring at their feet.

Frank's garden had looked dismal in the streetlight, his abandoned rose bushes leggy and unkempt, their last fallen petals turning brown as they rotted down into the earth. There was no car in the drive, no lights glowing from within the house. It could have been that Stella was in bed, which would have been the natural place to be at that hour, but Boyle didn't think so. The Valentine property had the dead look of an unlived-in home. Nobody breathing inside, nobody living there, laughing, eating, talking. Not even anybody dying there.

He wasn't surprised - hadn't expected to find her sitting there waiting for him, but however unlikely, there had been the kernel of hope. He'd had to try, and his options were limited, limited in fact to one. For all that he'd done because of her, for all that he'd loved and desired her, there was no other place he could start his search for Stella than the house she'd shared with Frank. He knew so much about her, and yet so little.

Boyle had tried the front door. It was locked, as expected. Knowing that no-one would answer, he rang the front door bell anyway, listening as it chimed emptily through the house. He walked around the building, checking the windows – all locked – and the back door – locked. No Stella, no nobody. The house was as dead as Frank.

Boyle stared at the blank windows as if staring long enough would give him the answers he needed. She could be anywhere, but wherever she was, he had to find her.

"Said she couldn't bear to stay in the house alone, too many memories," Dench said.

"Understandable, given the circumstances," Boyle swallowing his incredulity that Stella had confided in the wee man next door. "I don't suppose you know..."

"Somewhere in Perth – my wife has the details. Funny thing, I knew Frank quite well – we had the occasional round of golf together, but Mrs Valentine," Dench pursed his lips, "she wasn't one for... let's just say she liked to keep herself to herself, but then after Frank passed… well she called round, asked the wife and I to keep an eye on the place while she was away. Came across quite friendly – upset of course – she was distraught at the funeral. Big turn-out it was… Fine property, it will fetch a good price."

Boyle followed Dench's gaze and spent a moment with him staring at the For Sale sign outside Stella and Frank Valentine's house. She hadn't wasted any time in getting it on the market.

At Dench's invitation, Boyle walked with him and Bernice to his house. Boyle cranked up the charm, squeezing a dose of warmth into his smile as he was introduced to Mrs – call me Kitty – Dench. On hearing of his friendship with Frank and his night in the car, Call Me Kitty insisted that he stay for breakfast.

"I can't offer you a fry up – there's no bacon or sausages in this house - not since Bruce had his scare, but there's toast and porridge and I can do you poached eggs, if you like, Mr Grant."

"John, please - I insist."

He underlined his insistence with a touch on the arm and a side helping of twinkle.

"Would you like to freshen up, John?"

Boyle declined porridge and eggs but at Call Me's insistence, he made full use of the facilities. A stack of toast, a block of lightly salted butter and a pot of coffee were waiting for him after his shower, the price of which was an hour of Frank-related reminiscing with Mr Dench and a smattering of mild flirtation with his wife.

The pay-off was the address of the hotel where the Widow Valentine was doing her grieving.

Chapter 17

She filled his head, saturated his heart, she pulsed through his veins, wove her way through his nervous system. All he'd been doing these past two months was working hard at not thinking about her, but now the dam had been opened. *Stella, Stella, Stella.*

She had grey eyes. They could look blue or green depending on the light, cold or warm depending on her mood. And oh, the moods of the woman – she'd had him on a razor's edge right from the first time he'd laid eyes on her. Brittle one minute, soft and yielding as caramel the next. She'd sliced through skin, flesh, muscle, cutting him down to the bone. She'd welcomed him into her arms with a playful smile and caught him in a lethal embrace. She'd left permanent scars behind, but she was worth every excruciating second of pain.

Boyle felt as though he'd been holding his breath since September. All these weeks he'd been doing a good impersonation of being alive, but he'd been less than the sum of his parts. His skin doing nothing but keeping the rest of him in one place. But now he was alive. Rejuvenated, revitalised, resuscitated, reincar-bloody-nated. Now he could breathe and keep on breathing

He drove down the slip road onto the A9 and slapped his hand against the side of the steering wheel. Man, he was glad to be a part of the human race. If he was in a musical, he would have broken into song. *Zip-A-Dee-Bloody-Doo-Dah-Oh-What-A-Beautiful-Morning.*

Follow the yellow brick road all the way to the Broxden Roundabout at Perth. Follow, follow, follow the A9. The skies were leaden, the hills a drab shade of grey and an even drabber shade of brown and something else that was so nothing it wasn't even a colour. But Boyle was driving through a world painted in glorious Technicolor, trademark, copyright, with a song in his heart and a smile in his eyes. Everyone could see it. The kid in the back of the Renault he overtook could see it, the woman driving the Kia he zipped by could see it, hell, even the people on the opposite side of the carriageway could see it. They flashed their lights at him, sharing his *Zip-A-Dee-* Boyle glanced at the speedometer – *Doo-Dah*. Getting a little over-excited there, buddy.

He eased off, keeping an eye on the dial as it relaxed back to somewhere approaching the legal limit. He eased off some more, smiling as he passed the big white van with the speed camera sticking out the back. Ain't catching this fly in your trap.

No rush, he told himself. Even sticking to the limit, the journey wouldn't take him much more than a couple of hours. He eased off on the accelerator a little more and sure enough, the wheels kept turning and he got there in the end.

The hotel was an old Victorian dame hunkering down by the river. She had been given a face lift along with a new name and now the Fair City Hotel was all done out in neutral shades with splashes and swathes of extravagant purple.

Boyle picked a spot in the corner of the lounge that gave him a view of the front desk. Though he couldn't see the entrance from where he was sitting, there was enough of the lobby on show that he could see anyone waiting for the lift or going up the stairs. He ordered a coffee and waited.

He'd done a lot of waiting. Some of that waiting had been done in other hotels, in different places. Sometimes he'd been waiting for Stella. Sometimes it felt like he'd been waiting for her all of his life.

His coffee came with a disc of complimentary shortbread on the side. There was a pleasant buzz in the room, the new décor appealing to the coffee and cake brigade as well as the business meeter-uppers. Dark suits met in clumps, while the nattering chatters with their sleek hair, bright nails on the end of gesticulating hands, caught the eye like parakeets in flight, teeth, jewellery and eyes flashing. This was a latte-swilling-hot-yoga-cake-consuming human zoo.

Boyle picked up a newspaper left lying on a chair beside him and pretended to read it as he scoured the lobby. She could be in her room, up there all the while, maybe never leaving. Living off room-service, watching television in the dark, her hair-thinning, her colour fading. Didn't sound like Stella, but then what did?

He stretched his coffee all the way past lukewarm, down into cold, looking up every time he heard the swish of the revolving door or footsteps on the polished floor, but it was never her. Never Stella. The nattering chatters came, the nattering chatters went. The suits opened briefcases, made notes on phones, exchanged cards, shook hands, left.

"Can I get you anything else?" the waitress asked.

She hovered near him. She was young, maybe twenty, maybe younger, jaw length curly hair pinned back behind her ears, minimum make-up, wide-spaced eyes. Name tag on her décor-matching waistcoat.

"I was supposed to meet a friend," he said. "Looks like I've been stood up."

She threw him an expression he'd seen on a thousand faces, the half-twist of her lips about three streets away from a smile. *Why are you telling me this? I don't care about your sad, pathetic life. The only reason I'm not telling you to piss off is because I'm being paid to be nice to you.*

"She's staying here, blonde hair, green eyes…"

He caught a flash of recognition in the girl's eyes.

"Maybe you've seen her?" he asked.

Boyle smiled small, the waitress made a moue.

"Maybe," she shrugged.

She was on the brink. Tip her one way and she'd spill, tip her the other and hotel security would be escorting him off the premises.

Boyle sighed, "I may as well tell you the truth…" Spark of interest in those wide-set baby browns. "We had a bust-up. Hands up," he illustrated his words with the action, "I behaved like a dick – sorry – a fool." She smirked, letting him know she could handle language far fouler than dick. Tip, tip, tipping… "She walked out – I'll do anything to get her back. Truth is, Lisa, I'm lost without her."

Boyle completed the sigh-soliloquy combo with a full-on slumped shoulders, head-hanging, staring into the middle-distance, sad-sack routine. It would have brought tears to a glass eye, nearly brought one to his own, but Lisa's eyes were shrewd and she'd been working overtime on developing her seen-it-all veneer.

Boyle stared at Lisa's feet as he waited. Black pumps, scuffs on the toes, standing on carpet new enough not to have yet gained sticky patches and clots of dubious matter, but they would come with time. Criss-crossing shades of oatmeal, fawn and caramel flowed under tables, chairs, shoes, boots, sandals... tip, tip, tipping... which way, Lisa? Which way are you going to fall?

"Room 312."

Boyle looked up, "Thank you," he said.

Lisa cleared the table and brought the bill. Boyle left a tip twice what the coffee had cost. Room 312. He would go up there now, a-knocking on her door, Stella's door, his heart pitter-patting at the thought. He stood up and walked through the lounge, his feet a metre above the caramel river. He was floating on a love high. How could he ever have doubted his feelings for her?

As lounge carpet gave way to the heel-clacking tiled floor of the foyer, Boyle's phone chirped warning him of an incoming message. Still surfacing from the dreamy, caramel swirl, he took it from his pocket. Sudden switch from soft focus dream sequence to hard, close-up reality, every pore a crater, every twitch of the eye signifying seismic activity.

The message was from Jenny. Jenny his daughter. Jenny, the reason for him being here. Jenny whom he hadn't thought of, not once, since getting into Marilyn's *(who's she?)* car. It was all *Stella, Stella, Stella.*

The message read: *Tick tock Charlie*

Three photographs were attached. Boyle clicked on them, one after the other. The first showed someone running. A woman. Young, slender, long hair pulled back. The road lit by streetlights, her face indistinguishable. Boyle recognised the cut of the figure anyway. It was Jenny.

Second photograph, Jenny, closer, upper body shot, elbows bent at ninety degrees. Third photograph, Jenny's face. Up close, in the zone, running by the photographer, unaware of the lens focusing on her.

Unaware of the danger she was in.

Chapter 18

"Spill," Andrea said.

Jenny had hoped to pass through unannounced and unnoticed. The novelty of being in, of properly being part of the group was already wearing through. The welcoming warmth of friendship was in reality a suffocating heat. Being part of it meant constantly feeding the insatiable demand for information. She felt under pressure to give of herself, to open herself up in order to better reveal her innermost thoughts. And now – right now - when what she wanted most was to be by herself, to lick her wounds in private, they demanded that she take a knife to her belly and spill her guts so that they could pick over her entrails, savouring every last morsel of her rejection, her humiliation, her complete and utter getting-it-so-wrongness.

She'd already had a miserable day, dragging herself from lecture to lecture. A day of battling with her face, begging it not to betray her. She'd spent a lifetime covering up her feelings, considered herself well-versed in the art of revealing nothing of what was going on inside. Anyone would think she'd be skilled at it by now, but no, one glance from Andrea was all it took.

Andrea, with her unerring sense for emotional turmoil, fount of all relationship knowledge. And so she should be - she'd had enough of them, most of them the blink and you'll miss 'em sort, scarcely more than one-night-stands. *Don't be a bitch, she's your friend.* Yeah, but Jenny was on a roll and not in a mood for taking prisoners, the words tumbling around her head, expressing thoughts she didn't know she had until they leapt out fully formed.

Andrea considered a relationship long-term if it ran over two consecutive weekends. Her reward, a broken heart every couple or three months, followed by the statutory hump and dump debrief over a glass or six of prosecco, during which no detail was considered too small to be left out, no moment too private to be shared in the glare of the post mortem bitch fest.

She homed right in on Jenny's mood, wanting to know all, to savour the details before delivering her Delphic pronouncements over a glass – make that a bottle – of white. Any excuse for a drink, a gossip, a pretence at BestFriendsForever bullshit triteness with Kaz on her flank. Kaz with her I-am-so-wise, really got my shit together, shtick. Kaz, perfectly at ease in all social situations. Kaz, with her cute-yet-manly boyfriend. Kaz, Jenny's friend. Andrea, Jenny's friend. *Ever wished for something you got then wished you hadn't?*

Jenny mumbled something she couldn't even hear herself. An excuse of sorts, a jumble of vowels and consonants in no particular order. Countdown conundrum, go figure it out. Trying to get to her room before the she-wolves could pounce and drag it out of her, every last bit.

"C'mon, we know there's something up."

A touch on the arm. *Pounce.*

"Please, Jenny, don't block us out. We only want to help."

They had her by the metaphorical throat now. The pack was taking her down.

Next thing they were at the table. Coffee, not wine. Great steaming mugs of it. Coffee and conversation. Or interrogation. Depending on how you look at it.

It sounded so stupid when she said it out loud. So trite. She felt pathetic as every nuance of the date was picked over. A romantic meal. *Sounds like he's really into you.* That's what she thought. Cue sardonic laugh. Romantic meal followed by dismissal by taxi. *Dismissal? A bit abrupt perhaps, but not necessarily terminal.* Yeah, abrupt. Jenny's emotions (*lust*) left high and dry on a rock.

Have you called him?

Aye, there's the rub. Maybe she should have studied English Lit.

She told them about losing her phone. She couldn't remember his number and didn't know his address. Not that she would turn up on his doorstep. She wasn't a bunny boiler. She wasn't a stalker. She wasn't one of those untrusting, needy, please-be-nice-to-me, women. No, she wasn't one of those.

Then what was she?

"Why don't you just Facebook him?"

"He's not on Facebook."

They stared at her.

Jenny shrugged. "He doesn't do social media."

"Why don't you look his number up online?" Jenny and Andrea looked at Kaz and laughed.

Of course, it was so obvious. Though she didn't know his actual address, she knew he was in the Merchant City. There couldn't be too many *Killians, M.* in Glasgow. They checked the online directory.

This person could not be found.

The number you are searching for may be ex-directory.

"Or maybe he doesn't have a landline," Andrea said. "We don't."

"Or maybe he doesn't exist," Jenny replied.

Andrea screwed up her face. "Of course he exists, what are you talking about?"

"It's like Kaz said, I don't know anything about him-"

"I didn't mean-" Kaz backtracking, not wanting to be right, not if it meant she had to witness Jenny's humiliation.

Jenny's interior voice berated her for being such a bitch before, for having doubts that these women were her friends. Real and actual.

"It's true," she said, "he appeared from nowhere. Maybe it's just as well he's disappeared again. Maybe I've had a lucky esc-"

The opening up, the revealing, the bleeding, cut short by the sound of the entry buzzer. Looks exchanged three ways. *Expecting anyone?*

It was Andrea who got up, went to the intercom but it was Jenny's heart pounding as the voice came through, tinny, hollow but unmistakably his.

Hi, my name's Michael, I'm looking for Jenny. Jenny Boyle.

Chapter 19

The eager beaver look on Jenny's face when he walked through the door killed him. He couldn't have managed it better if he'd been writing the script. The blonde and the red-head made their excuses and scarpered, but only after the blonde – Kaz – checked if Jenny was okay to be left alone with him.

Killian sent the blonde a smile that would have charmed a cobra but she didn't fall for it. Judging by the look she shot right back at him her blood ran way cooler than reptile but her instincts were shit-hot. Killian was all kinds of bad and she knew it. That made her a problem.

He made a mental note on the blonde and tucked it away for future reference. Right now his focus was all on Jenny.

He sat across the table from her, the silence between them emphasised by low fidelity background sounds. Doors opening and closing, the click of light switches, faint sounds of music playing.

Jenny stared into an empty mug while he stared at her. Sweet little Jenny. Hurting her would be like kicking a kitten, but then Killian never did like cats.

"Why haven't you been returning my calls?" he asked.

She looked up at him. The confusion on her face was tasty. He'd like to have taken a moment to savour it but there was more work to be done.

"I thought it was going really well between us," he worked the hurt look, "but if you don't want to see me again you could do me the favour of letting me know. You could at least have sent a text. Don't just blank me out of your life, Jenny."

He racked up the intensity as he talked until he was emoting like a pub singer giving it Whitney. This was his journey and he was owning it.

"I thought we had something." He turned his head away, biting the inside of his lips to stop him from cracking up.

"Michael — I haven't been ignoring your calls — I lost my phone." Her voice a candy swirl of hope and bewilderment.

He looked back at her, his face wide open, eyebrows raised — had all of this… could it possibly be… a misunderstanding?

"You lost…?"

"Yes," she nodded, a faint smile of hope ghosting her lips. "I lost my phone — I didn't know how to get in touch with you."

"I thought…"

"No," she shook her head.

"Then we're all right then?"

"Yes," a real smile dawned rendering her face all teeth and sparkling eyes.

He mentally gave himself a high five. Baby, he'd brought it all the way home and she'd bought it wholesale, no need for a receipt.

He'd prepped her and tenderised her. Now it was time to get out the knives.

Chapter 20

The carpet was deeper in this section of corridor, the wallpaper – segregated from standard fare by fire doors – was so on trend it would be out with the ark in six months. Room 312 was on the side with a river view and no doubt came with complimentary extras - bath robes, slippers, bottled water, and a wee packet of shortbread in a tartan wrapper. Though it was hardly a five-star luxury joint, Boyle appreciated the fact that the Fair City Hotel was a trier. It was certainly a couple of rungs up the ladder from most of the places he had dossed in over the past couple of months.

He stood to the side of the door, back against the wall and took a few deep breathes to calm his nerves. It was a cigarette kind of moment and if he'd been offered one there and then, he'd have taken it. He'd have sucked that blue smoke right down his trachea, through his bronchi and into the deepest recesses of his lungs. Taking the nicotine hit, getting the old familiar comfort. He wondered if she still smoked. Thought maybe she only ever had because Frank detested it so.

Time now. Boyle rapped on the door and uttered the classic line, "Room service."

He listened hard and was rewarded by soft sounds of movement. The stirring of a body, the whisper of fabric. The sudden appearance of light filtering through the crack at the bottom of the door caught his eye. Whatever she'd been doing in there, she'd been doing it in the dark. A shadow thrown broke the bright line as she walked across the room towards him. Now, after weeks, days, hours of separation, all that stood between Boyle and Stella was one lousy hotel door.

Boyle stood square on his side of the barrier. If she looked through the fish eye she'd see him large as life, twice as ugly. Didn't matter, not now. She had no place to run and he wasn't going anywhere. If she didn't open up, he'd give it some Big Bad and huff and puff and break his way in.

Settle down, Charlie. You're getting ahead of yourself. No need for aggression.

A clink and a clank and Stella opened up, and when she opened, she opened wide.

"Hello, Charlie. What took you so long?"

Chapter 21

Kaleidoscope colours she could almost taste, smiles exploding on faces, laughter flowing unfettered from lips, lights shining brighter, blood flowing warmer - falling in love was like riding a crazy carousel. Round and round and up and down, until she was giddy. Until it almost didn't feel real. And yet it was real, because there Michael was, right in front of her, his eyes as glittery as hers felt. They were locked in on each other. Nothing else mattered. The rest of the world didn't exist. There was only the two of them, cocooned in warmth and light. And love. Love – she played the word over and over in her head. This was what love felt like.

"Smile," Michael said.

As if she wasn't smiling enough already, but Jenny was eager to please. She stretched it until her lips bruised as she laughed into the lens of his phone.

"I want photographs," he said. He looked into her eyes, through them, beyond what was revealed to the rest of the world. His gaze lit a fuse, igniting Catherine wheels, roman candles, rockets and strobes inside her. "Lots of photographs - to look at when I'm not with you. I want to be able to see you, Jenny. Always."

That he felt as she did was the best of it and yet the intensity was almost unbearable. In that moment, Jenny felt that it was possible to spontaneously combust. That the two of them could ignite, their flames whooshing into the night sky, returning their elements to the stars. *Carbon, hydrogen, oxygen*.

"You feel it too, don't you?"

Gazing into his eyes, into the wondrous universes contained therein. "Yes, Michael. I feel it too." *Nitrogen, calcium, phosphorus*.

He wanted to be with her always, but still he left. The real world intruding, pulling him away. This time though, it did not feel like a rejection, it was simply life. He hadn't known what to expect when he came to her door, did not know if she would even agree to see him. That she had, that their encounter had gone better than he could ever have hoped… well, he hadn't been prepared for that. He couldn't have stood to set himself up for the fall, he said. It would have broken him.

They had moved on to a new level, but the rest of the world was exactly where it had been before. He had work to catch up on. Something to do with a report he could not put off. It had seemed clear when he was explaining to her, but now the details were hazy. So hazy, she wasn't entirely sure what it was he had to do or why. It hardly mattered – it wasn't a job interview, it was love and nothing else mattered.

He had gone and she was on the sofa, arms wrapped around an overstuffed cushion, hugging it because she had to squeeze some energy out somehow or she would explode. She felt like dancing, no running – she felt like running. She felt that she could run for miles and miles and miles-

A rat-a-tat-tat on the door snapped her back to the here and now. Michael had work to deal with. She had flatmates. The door opened before she could respond, Andrea's head appearing around it.

"Is he gone? Can we come in?"

Andrea piled in like a party arriving. Her laughter shrunk back a little at the sight of Kaz looking like she was shredding her tongue on a Soor Ploom.

"Jenny, you sly dog - he is gorgeous. Tell all, c'mon – it's good news isn't it?"

Andrea flopped on the sofa beside her. Kaz sat at the table.

"C'mon, spill," Andrea nudged her.

"Okay, okay. It was all a big misunderstanding."

"So you guys are… together?"

Jenny nodded like a bobble-head. "Yes, we're together." Andrea squealed and hugged her. Jenny glanced over Andrea's shoulder at Kaz. She was holding back on smiles like happiness was rationed.

"What's up?" Jenny asked when Andrea finally released her.

Kaz looked at the ceiling, the walls, her hands, anywhere but Jenny. The longer she didn't look at Jenny the more riled Jenny became.

"Aw, c'mon Kaz, what's the problem?" Andrea asked.

Andrea was, Jenny knew, looking for an excuse to crack open a bottle of wine. Jenny meeting her true love – in fact Jenny having any kind of social life at all – was more than enough reason and Andrea did not take well to Kaz putting a downer on the promised party.

Finally, Kaz steeled herself and looked at Jenny. "How much do you really know about this guy, Jenny?"

"C'mon Kaz, lighten up." Andrea said. "If I didn't know you better, I'd say you had a touch of the green-eyes."

Andrea laughed - it was a joke, *get it?* – but Kaz's face hardened.

"Jealous?" she asked. "Of that guy? I don't think so."

Jenny sat up straight and jutted her jaw. "What do you mean – *of that guy?*"

"Jenny, can't you see it? He's a... he's a player."

Jenny pushed the cushion aside. If she'd never bristled before, she was bristling now, and how. *Spikey, spike, spike.*

"What do you mean, *a player?* You don't know anything about him."

"Maybe not, but then neither do you."

"Whoa, steady now, girls." Andrea raised her hands, palms out. "Getting a bit heated in here, let's say we turn it down a notch."

Kaz sucked in a breath. "Okay, listen - I'm sorry... I went too far."

"Good, that's good," Andrea nodded like she was spouting the Wisdom of Solomon.

She placed a hand on the back of Jenny's shoulder, a conciliatory gesture that annoyed the hell out of Jenny. She stood up, her insides knotting.

"I'm not jealous, really I'm not," Kaz said.

Jenny stared at her. Smart, beautiful, Kaz – she had it all going on. Sporty boyfriend, switched-on social life, making all the right connections, at ease with herself and her place in the world, and yet here she was having a pop at Jenny. But in a *caring* way. Jenny wanted to slap her.

"Jenny, please sit down so that we can talk."

"It's good to talk," Andrea said.

Jenny looked at Andrea sideways, wondering – not for the first time - if she had cheese for brains.

"Tell you what, I'll open a bottle of white and we can sit down and sort this thing out, all friends together."

Andrea got up and went to the fridge. Once she had the idea of a glass of wine in her head, she was never going to let it go. She put the bottle on the table along with three glasses then looked at Jenny.

"Please," Kaz said.

Jenny considered walking away. She didn't need this. She certainly didn't want it. But where would that leave her? Living in an atmosphere, both feet out of the social soup. Just living on a day-to-day basis would be seventeen kinds of awkward. Why put herself through that when all she had to do was sit.

She sat.

Nobody spoke until Andrea glugged wine into the glasses.

"Well, this is nice," Andrea faked a jolly face. "All of us, here, together. Drinking wine."

Filling the gaps. Greasing the social wheels.

"I'm happy you're happy, really I am," Kaz, all earnest. Being a *true* friend. "I just wish it was… someone else."

"What's wrong with Michael?" Jenny's voice tight. Her mouth all puckered up like she'd been sucking on a lemon.

"There's something about him… it's hard to put my finger on, but he's not right. At least he's not right for you." Kaz paused, perhaps expecting Jenny to say something. When Jenny remained silent, Kaz ploughed on, getting herself in good and deep. "You've been all over the place since you met him. Sky-high one minute, hitting the deck the next. You thought he'd dumped you last night and now the big romance is back on."

The muscles in Jenny's face tightened as she listened, but she kept her mouth shut. Let the Perfect One say her piece before she choked on it.

"Anyone for a top-up?" Andrea splashed wine into each of the glasses though she was the only one drinking.

"Go on," Jenny's voice strangling her vocal chords as she addressed Kaz.

"There's something off," Kaz said. "You lost your phone and had no way of getting in contact with him – no address, no landline, no place of work – but he knew where you lived and turned up on your doorstep. He came out of nowhere, Jenny. You don't know anything about him, but he knows plenty about you. It's all out of kilter."

Jenny stared at Kaz, waiting to see if there was more. The silence grew fat. Even Andrea was weighed down, unable to raise her glass, until Jenny finally punctured it.

"That all you've got?"

Kaz nodded. Credit where it was due – she did look miserable. And so she deserved to be. She hadn't just rained on Jenny's parade - she'd spewed all over it. Jenny came out fighting.

"The only thing that's out of kilter is you. I had no idea you had such a twisted world view, Kaz. Michael knows where I live because he dropped me off before. And I know plenty about him – in fact, I know everything I need to know."

"I'm sorry, Jenny. I didn't mean to upset you – it's just that… I don't trust him."

"*Trust him?*" Jenny felt as though her head was about to explode. "You don't *need* to trust him. You don't *need* to have anything to do with him. What are you – my mother?"

"No, I'm your friend."

"Some friend. And while we're at it – how come your instincts count for more than mine?"

"They don't, really, Jenny. I just don't want you to get hurt."

"I'm not going to get hurt. Michael loves me – and I love him."

"Love? You've only just met the guy."

"Oh good grief – you really are my mother, aren't you? What did you do – swallow her whole with a side order of sanctimony?"

"Jenny…" Kaz, pleading.

"Kaz, you know what – I don't need this. Seriously, there must be a big hole in your own life if you're so over-invested in mine."

Jenny stood up and stalked off, Kaz and Andrea bleating at her back. *Come back, sit down, don't go, let's talk…* She got some satisfaction from slamming the door behind her, but it was hardly enough. Some friend Kaz was. Who'd have thought she'd turn out to be such a bitch? She should be happy that Jenny was happy. Maybe Andrea was right, maybe she was jealous – many a true word and all that. Maybe things weren't as they appeared with her and the wonderful Nick.

Whatever. Looked like she had one less friend in the world than she thought. Didn't matter – none of it mattered. Not Andrea with her stupid, endless partying. Not the practically perfect Kaz with her if-I-was-chocolate-I-would-eat-myself boyfriend.

The only thing that did matter was that she and Michael had found each other. Maybe she hadn't known him for long – but how long did a person need? Jenny already knew everything she needed to know and it all boiled down to one thing.

Michael was the one.

Chapter 22

Whatever Boyle had been expecting, this wasn't it.

Stella turned and walked back into the room. Boyle closed the door behind him and followed, the way he always did. What else was there to do?

The room turned out to be a suite. They were in a small lounge. An open arch led to the bedroom. As the sky darkened, she'd been sitting by the window, watching the lights twinkle on the Tay.

"It's pretty, isn't it?" she said.

"It sure is," Boyle replied.

But Boyle wasn't looking through the window. He didn't give a damn about rivers and lights and what the hell. All the view he needed was standing right in front of him. He hadn't known how thirsty he was but when he saw her he realised – he'd been trekking through a desert in the midday sun. He was dying of thirst but now he drank her in, long and deep. Impossible though it seemed, she was more beautiful than he remembered.

She'd had her hair cut shorter. It was soft and tousled. He liked the way it curled at her neck. She'd lost a little weight, but she still went in and out in all the right places. It was the way she held herself that caught him. She didn't seem so… brittle. Stella had grey eyes. They could look blue or green depending on the light. Cold or warm, depending on her mood. When she turned to him now they were warm and green.

"I've missed you, Charlie."

Even if his life depended on it, Boyle couldn't say who moved first, and he didn't care. All that mattered was that Stella was in his arms again. Holding him as tight as he was holding her. He inhaled her perfume, breathing it in deep. It was fresh and light like a spring breeze. He nuzzled her hair and kissed her neck before their lips met. No taste of cigarettes and coffee, not this time. She tasted the way a warm summer day felt.

The feel of her against him, her smell, her touch, transported him to the dream he'd once had of them together, blue skies stretching forever overhead, warm, golden sand beneath bare feet, the sound of lapping waves. Living simply, living well, the two of them in the sun. Now, even as they stripped the clothes from each other, sighing and moaning as fabric whispered to the floor, the dream felt within his grasp.

They swayed in time to the music playing in his head, keeping such a perfect rhythm as they waltzed slowly to the bedroom that Boyle wondered if she could hear it too.

The tempo changed as they fell on the bed. Already half-naked, they tore the remaining clothes from themselves and each other. He wanted to feel her, every part of her. Skin against skin, flesh merging into flesh, muscles flexing, her mouth against his ear, moaning as his fingers explored the sweet spot between her legs.

He responded as she pushed and manipulated him until he was on his back, Stella sitting astride him. Slowly she lowered herself onto him. He gasped as she arched her back, her breasts quivering in the demi-light as the two of them became one.

From the crumpled heap of his clothes in the other room came the muffled sound of his phone. Its call so distant, he could pretend it wasn't there at all.

Afterwards they lay on their backs breathing heavily, skin slick with sweat, the top sheet tangled around their lower limbs, the duvet spilling from the bed, pooling on the floor. Lying apart as they cooled and recovered, the only part of their bodies now touching were their legs - his right partially against her left, keeping the connection.

When she'd recovered sufficiently, or perhaps because she felt exposed in the aftermath of their feverish coupling, Stella retrieved the sheet and billowed it over them. Boyle smiled as the fabric settled, contouring his body.

"Hello Stella," he said.

"Hello Charlie."

"How you been?"

"Okay, I guess. You?"

"Surviving, Stella. I've been surviving."

Boyle rolled on his side and propped himself up on his elbow, head resting in his hand. She looked at him. Her hair was all mussed up. He traced his fingers along her collar bone.

"It's been hard without you, baby." Her skin ran smooth and fine over the slender curve of her clavicle.

"What took you so long?"

"I'd have got here sooner if I knew you were waiting, but how was I to know? You ran out on me, Stella."

"I didn't run out on you, Charlie. I saved you."

"Yeah?" Boyle raised an eyebrow.

"Yeah. Feels like forever I've been waiting."

"You could have let me in on the plan."

"I couldn't... you had to believe we were over – that I'd run out on you - or it wouldn't have worked, but I knew that sooner or later that brain of yours would slip into gear and you'd figure out. That you would come looking."

He ran his fingers to her shoulder and stopped. "Stella, are you feeding me a line?"

She sighed. "Charlie, will you ever trust me?"

"I want to trust you, baby. Truly I do, but you stung me big time."

She took hold of his hand, bent her head and kissed his fingers. "Did I hurt you, Charlie?"

"Yeah, Stella. You hurt me."

"There's a lot of it around."

He pulled his hand free from her grasp. "Tell me the truth, Stella."

Are you serious? Do we really have to do this?"

"Yeah, I'm serious. Spill."

"Okay, I'll spell it out."

"Loud and clear, baby."

Some of it stacked. The warm welcome had seemed genuine enough, but he knew how good a fake Stella could be. But here was the rub – he wanted to believe her. More than anything, he wanted to believe.

"How hard was it to find me? Come on, Charlie – how hard? I could have been anywhere in the country – anywhere in the world – but you found me here, didn't you? I bet you hardly even had to use those old detective skills of yours, did you?"

Boyle closed his eyes and groaned. "Dench," he said.

"Got it in one, Charlie. Good old Mr Dench and his busybody wife. Telling them was like taking out a full-page ad. I knew that you'd trip over Mr and Mrs Dench sooner or later – that is if you were serious about finding me."

"How long have you been here?" he asked.

"Weeks, Charlie. I've been killing time for weeks. Life on pause. One day merging into the next, thinking about everything that happened, wondering what was keeping you. What did keep you – what were you up to?"

"Up to?" Boyle shrugged. "Nothing. I've been doing nothing but drifting."

"You do any thinking while you were drifting?"

"Not if I could help it."

"So why now – why are you here now?"

When he said he hadn't been doing any thinking, Boyle had been telling the truth, but he was thinking plenty now – and fast.

"Listen Stella, if I'd known you were waiting I'd have come sooner, but I didn't know – I thought you wanted me out, I thought you'd set me up – that my get out of jail free card was a happy by-product of you ripping me off. In fact, I've been doing everything I could not to think about you. I was scared that if I did, it would tear me up inside… and there's not much of me left to tear up, Stella. I'm all hollowed out. Dead man walking."

"So why now – why this moment?"

Boyle rolled onto his back. He lay with his arm crooked, back of his hand on his forehead, and stared at the ceiling.

Stella got up on her elbow and stared at him. "Charlie?"

He turned his head and looked at her from beneath his arm. "The diamonds, Stella. I need the diamonds."

"Oh."

She gave him that one syllable before getting up, the tone of her voice as flat as the look in her eyes before she turned away from him. She went into the bathroom, the door closing sharply behind her. Boyle lay in the demi-dark and stared at the ceiling. Thinking, he was still thinking. Mainly he was thinking that he could have handled the situation better. A lot better.

He was still lying there when she emerged, a white towel wrapped around her body. Her hair all turbaned up in another. She flicked on a lamp. He watched her sidewise as she fussed around opening and closing drawers, taking things out, putting things back. She didn't know what the hell she was doing.

Suddenly she stopped and turned to him. "Was it just the diamonds, Charlie, or do you feel anything for me at all?"

He sat up. "It's all about you Stella, baby. It has always been about you. I told you – I'd have been here like a shot if I'd known you wanted me. Thing is, I don't have any extra sensory powers, you know. I'm not psychic, Stella. I thought we were done… You don't make it easy for a guy."

The sight of her standing there staring at him, swathed in white, her skin glowing in the lamp light, sent quivers through him.

"No," she said. "I don't suppose I do."

"The diamonds… they're not for me."

Tiny tics in her face, muscles working in her brow, around her eyes, at the corners of her mouth, told him of scepticism, of questions going through her mind.

"If not you… then who?"

The question was obvious. Trouble was, the minute Boyle let Stella flood his mind, he managed to forgot all about the who – "Oh shit!"

He flung back the sheet and made a dash to the clothes lying in a heap. He scrabbled through them, looking for his phone. *How could he forget?* Stella, Stella, it was all about Stella, except it wasn't. Quaint though the thought was, other people did actually exist. Trouble was, whenever he was around her or even thinking about her it didn't seem that way. It was just Stella, filling him, taking him over.

He extracted the phone. There was a message – from Jenny. Or at least from the phone which had been Jenny's. Boyle opened it. Two words appeared on the screen.

tick tock

Boyle opened the attachment. It was another photograph of Jenny. This one close up. She was laughing, looking right at the camera. She had the kind of look on her face little kids got on Christmas morning when they saw a heap of presents under the tree. The message may have been wrapped up in smiles and laughter, but Boyle understood the true meaning. Boyle's past had caught up on him and caught up good.

Stella came up behind him and looked at the screen over his shoulder.

"Who is she?"

Chapter 23

"I need the diamonds, Stella."

"Sure you do, Charlie."

She'd pulled on a pair of jeans and a cashmere sweater that clung to her curves and begged to be touched if only to prove how soft it was. It was a high maintenance article of clothing, requiring hand washing and reshaping whilst damp. Boyle wished he could be reshaped. Stella had already hung him out to dry and now she was taking him to the cleaners.

"Jenny's in trouble."

"Sure she is, Charlie," Stella glanced again at the laughing image on Boyle's phone, "right up to her slender white throat by the look of things."

"I swear it, Stella. They're holding her to ransom."

Stella raised an eyebrow.

"Well then it looks as though she's got a serious case of Stockholm Syndrome."

"I mean it, Stella. They've got her... she just doesn't know it yet."

It was like trying to prove yourself sane in a psychiatric unit. Stella looked at him the way a person would regard the dark matter clogging a sink hole. It was a look that curled up his insides and fizzed his brain. How the hell could he convince her that he was telling the truth? He worked his mouth hoping the right words would flow but Stella was already unleashing a rant.

"Way to go, Charlie. You know you didn't have to go fabricating your ludicrous tales, and you didn't need to screw me. You could at least have been honest with me and come right out with it. All you want – all you ever wanted – were the diamonds. Hard stones for a hard heart. No – wait a minute – I take that back. You don't have a heart, Charlie. Nobody with a heart could use their daughter the way you just did."

"I know what it looks like, but I'm telling you the truth."

"It looks like she's having the time of her life and you've

been caught out in a-"

"It is the truth, Stella."

She turned away from him as if she couldn't bear to look at him a second longer. Riled by the dismissal Boyle snatched out and caught her by the hand. The fine bones of her metacarpals rolled in his grasp, which was harder and tighter than he'd intended. She yelped. Aghast, Boyle released her. She took a swing at him. He caught her by the wrist. The unleashed fury of the intended slap unfurled on her face as Stella snarled at him like an alley cat.

The punch came unseen. A fist smashed into the side of Boyle's face, knocking him off balance, sending him stumbling and reeling into an occasional table. Time did its elastic trick and as he fell with all the grace of a sack of coal he had time to wonder what the hell had just happened. He landed in an ungraceful heap beside the lamp he'd caught with his arm during his flight. He sat up in a tangle of lightshade and wire feeling like the definition of perplexed. Heat radiated from the spot where the unknown fist had connected with his face. He flexed his jaw and felt for damage. A pair of grey chukka boots appeared before him.

"Broken?"

Boyle's gaze followed the denim clad legs above the boots to a navy Harrington jacket. From above the jacket a face looked down upon him the features of which had bedded in, twenties softness gone, hard edged forties still over the horizon. His blonde hair was buzz cut, number two all over. Boyle pitched him at thirty-two, give or take. Looked like Buzz had been doing a lot of work on the hard stare. Or maybe he was the genuine article. He'd have the chance to prove himself either way soon enough.

Boyle dabbled at his jaw then wiggled it. "Nah, don't think so –"

"Pity."

Boyle looked from Buzz to Stella and back again. She wasn't giving anything away. "Hard man," Boyle said.

"Get up and I'll show you who's hard."

Boyle pushed the lamp aside and got up. Fair dos, Buzz waited until he was square on his feet before taking another swing at him. Boyle dodged the punch and swung one of his own, and so they danced on, feinting and swiping, banging into furniture and working up a sweat until Buzz ripped Boyle's gut with a shovel hook. Boyle doubled over and let out an oof, thinking that was it, the game was a bogey.

"That's enough," Stella's voice cut through the pain.

No way would her command be enough to save Boyle's pretty features. Buzz's blood was up. He was all set to pound Boyle's head to mince and Boyle was set to take it. Sometimes that was just the way it was. But lo – the pummelling did not come.

When Boyle stopped feeling like he was going to throw up his liver, he straightened up and got his mouth working.

"Who the hell are you?" he asked Buzz.

Buzz stared at him like he was stupid. "Elmer," he said.

"As in Fudd?" Boyle asked.

"As in Gantry," Elmer replied. "Wanna make something of it?"

"Not particularly," Boyle said, "but I'm none the wiser."

"Elmer Gantry – Burt Lancaster film. My mother was a fan."

"So why didn't she name you Burt?"

"I don't know, why don't you ask her?"

Elmer's face went tight as a fist. Looked like Boyle was going to be minced after all. The way he was feeling, he just wanted it over and done with. They could put him in a box when Elmer was done with him, tie it up with a pink ribbon and toss the whole damn package into the river.

"Settle down," Stella said to Elmer, and to Boyle, "he's my brother."

Boyle gaped a little and looked back and forth between them. Come to mention it, there was something of a resemblance.

"Brother? I didn't know you had a brother."

"I'm the family's dirty little secret," Elmer said.

"He's one of them at any rate," Stella said. "Same father, different mothers."

"So what's he doing here?"

That was the question Boyle asked out loud. Inside he was wondering what else he didn't know about Stella.

"He was going to help me sell the diamonds."

"You told him?"

"You weren't around - I had to tell someone."

"What does he know?"

"I am here you know," Elmer said. "And F.Y.I. – I know everything."

Boyle looked at Stella. "Everything?"

"Yeah, that'll be everything - Charlie," Elmer replied.

Boyle looked back at Elmer. Elmer winked. "Frank was an arsehole," he said. "He got what was coming to him."

"That's pretty harsh."

"Life's harsh."

"Who were you going to sell them to?" Boyle asked.

"I got connections."

"Yeah?"

"Yeah."

"Connect with this then." Boyle's fist introduced itself to Elmer's gut. Now it was Elmer's turn to oof. Boyle had to admit, it felt pretty good being the one dishing out the surprises for a change.

Stella put her arm across Elmer's back. "Are you okay?" she asked. Elmer nodded. Stella looked up at Boyle. "What did you do that for?"

"He had it coming," Boyle said. "Don't worry, he'll get over it."

He made to assist Elmer in his recovery. No bad feelings and all that, but Stella told him to back off.

"Oh sure," Boyle said. "I'll back off alright – just as soon as I get the diamonds."

"You know," she said, "I feel like a fool – I really thought you came for me."

"You feel like a fool? I thought you were waiting for me

– but it turns out you were just waiting for Elmer here to make his connection."

Elmer straightened up beside Stella.

"That's not true Charlie – I was waiting for you the whole time – remember Mr Dench?"

"How could I forget? Yeah, Mr Dench – a portrait in beige – is he in on it too?"

"Mr Dench? Don't be ridiculous."

"You're calling me ridiculous? You're the one who is all set to hand over the diamonds to Elmer Fudd, here."

"Don't call me that," Elmer said.

"Go shoot a wabbit," Boyle replied.

Elmer lunged at him, but this time Boyle was prepared. He took a neat sidestep. "Take it easy, Elmer. I'm toying with you."

"Lay off, Charlie," Stella told him.

"I will lay off, but first I need the diamonds –"

"Oh yes, your daughter – she's in mortal danger, isn't she?"

"Actually, yeah she is… Listen Stella, straight up – remember Sammy?"

"That's the guy you killed, right?" Elmer said.

Boyle looked from Stella to Elmer and back. Felt like his mouth was hanging open.

"I told you," she said, "I told him everything."

"Jesus wept."

"That he surely did," Elmer said.

Boyle took some time out to gape at him before continuing. "Yeah, right, so it turns out that Sammy was only doing the job to pay off a debt – a big one – and the guy he owes wants paying – by me. It's true, Stella – whatever you think of me, Jenny really is in danger. She just doesn't know it yet, and I have no way of warning her. I need the diamonds. You've got to believe me."

Stella and Elmer stared at him for what seemed a long time. For all he knew they were conversing telepathically. Whatever they were up to, he wasn't in on it. Mountain ranges could have formed in the time they were standing there, but finally Stella spoke.

"Okay Charlie, I believe you."

Boyle sighed. Progress at last. "Great, thanks – I mean it, but I still need the diamonds."

"They're not here," Stella said.

"Well where are they then?"

Stella and Elmer exchanged glances. More telepathic shit going down. Boyle didn't like it. Made him feel like he'd unwittingly taken a stroll into Midwich. It was Elmer who finally spoke up.

"They're at our father's place."

Boyle stared at the pair of them until his eyeballs were ready to pop. "What is this – a family affair?"

They said nothing.

Boyle's left temporal artery pulsed.

Chapter 24

Friel's daughter drifted by as he walked through the front door. He said hello, but she was plugged in, her ears full of whatever was playing on her iPod, her gaze on the glowing screen, lost in a world from which he was excluded. She wandered into her bedroom and closed the door behind her, oblivious to his presence. Or perhaps choosing not to acknowledge it.

"Debs?" Friel called his wife's name. There was no response.

He hung his coat in the closet then walked through to the open plan living area of the penthouse. A magnet held a note to the front of a refrigerator large enough to house a couple of loosely packed corpses.

Out with Val. Dinner in fridge. Debs x

Friel scowled. Who the hell was Val? He scratched at the memory of a recent conversation. Val… new stylist in the Duke Street salon? He thought Debs didn't like her – she got the customers' backs up. Or was that Yvonne?

He opened the fridge. Right at the front, on the eye level shelf, was a ready meal with a post-it note attached – *Lenny - dinner*. He removed the box and peeled off the note. Vegetarian cottage pie made with soya and lentils. Christ almighty, the woman was taking the piss and then some. Friel chucked the box back into the fridge and had a rummage for something edible.

There was enough of Debs' prosecco in there to float a battleship but food-wise it was bags of organic greenery and tubs of salad from Marks and Spencer. There wasn't as much as a pack of sliced ham or chicken wings to be had, never mind a pork pie. He never should have let her come with him when he'd had that check-up. The quack had uttered those two fateful words, *high cholesterol*, and Friel's fate was sealed. No wonder his blood pressure was rocketing. It was a load of crap. She could come to the doctor with him, but she was never here when he got in at night.

Friel swung the fridge door shut and poured himself a large malt. He should have stopped for a white pudding supper on the way home. That would have shown her. Except she wasn't here to be shown. He wanted her here. She used to always be here, pouring his drink, massaging his shoulders. He took his phone out. He would call her, tell her to come home – no, he knew her. Telling her to come home wouldn't go down well, especially if she was in a party mood. She'd called him a boring old fart too many times lately, and if he came the heavy hand he'd be getting nothing but hot tongue and cold shoulder for weeks to come. He had to play it smart and make her an offer she couldn't refuse. The casino. That would get her going.

Friel fixed a smile on his face and pressed call. It went straight to voicemail. He tossed the phone on the counter and took his drink over to the floor-to-ceiling window. He gazed out at the cityscape spread before him. Sodium streetlights glowed yellow under an inky black sky. Govan was just a mile downstream on the other side of the Clyde. It wasn't far in terms of distance, but in every other way Lenny Friel had travelled a million miles from the back courts of the tenements where he grew up.

A person couldn't get peace and quiet back then. Not like now. There was plenty of quiet all around him now. The flat felt empty, with too much quiet and precious little peace. He stared along the river towards his old stomping ground. The stone stairs in the close where he lived had been bevelled from years of weary footsteps, the steep ascent lit by gas mantles. It was like something out of an old film, but it wasn't an old film, it was his life.

It had been hard graft to get from there to here and it irked him that his daughter wasn't grateful for the privileged life she led. Her utter disdain for him irked him even more. If eye-rolling had been an Olympic sport, she'd have been a gold medallist. But in many ways he was proud that she took her comfortable life for granted. That she had never known anything else was a testament to his success. He doubted she'd ever seen rats scavenging in a midden, in fact she'd probably didn't know what a midden was.

The ring of his phone interrupted Friel's musings. Debs, returning his call. Maybe it wasn't too late to salvage the night. He went back to the counter and picked it up. Bobby Big Cheeks' name was on the screen. Friel had only left him a couple of hours ago. He answered and listened, the scowl lines around his eyes deepening as Bobby spoke.

The word was out. The whisper on the street was that Friel had gone soft. He'd let a clown like Sammy Macallister take the piss and now there were people moving in on his territory in the north of the city. They were selling drugs – luring customers in with special introductory deals. Loansharking with a smile, undercutting Friel's rates. They were skirting around the edges just now, but it wouldn't be long before they were pushing in.

"Sort it out," Friel spoke though tight, bloodless lips. "Find out who they are and put an end to it – no holds barred. I want bones broken. I want teeth knocked out. I want their blood running in the gutters. You hear?"

Bobby told him that he heard. A sound in the background caught Friel's attention. A murmuring voice.

"What's that?"

"Nothing, I'm in the street, just someone passing."

Friel hung up. Rage bubbled within him but he kept a lid on it. He'd fought long, hard and dirty to get where he was and he would not lose control now. He would not lose anything. He knew there was more to this game than brute force. It wasn't just battering the other guy that mattered, it was having him scared of you battering him. Fear was what motivated people, and when they stopped being scared they stopped being motivated.

A house of cards was what it was. If they lost faith in his ability to terrorise, the whole façade came tumbling down. His success depended on other people believing that the worst thing that could happen to them was getting on the wrong side of Lenny Friel.

It was the *thought* of broken bones and burst-up faces that scared people. Public Relations was where it was at. He had to send out the right message, and then he had to keep reinforcing it so that people would not only believe, but keep the faith.

He scrolled through the contacts on his phone until he found the name he wanted and pressed call.

Michael Killian answered on the second ring.

"Where's Boyle?"

"I'm reeling him in," Killian replied.

"You're not listening – I want him now. Step it up and step it up fast. You do whatever it takes, but I want him and I want the stones."

A pause, just a heart-beat in length. Time enough for Friel to narrow his eyes.

"You'll get him."

"Don't let me down, Michael."

Friel hung up. He looked at the window again, his gaze now focussed on the glass rather than through it. A hollow-eyed image of himself stared back, mouth set in a grim line.

Friel prided himself on being a thoughtful man, a reflective man. He wasn't just some back street thug, a tuppence ha'penny hooligan. He'd have been all washed up years ago if that had been the case. A has-been, full of stories of the glory days, boring the arse off of anyone he could latch onto in the pub about how he used to be someone. Picking up crumbs from the big men's table like a scabby, half-cocked pigeon.

He was no sucker, he was smart, switched-on. He had the brains and the balls. He was the man. The main man. He was top dog, A-Number-One, and he'd rip out the spine of anyone who said otherwise. Or better still, have someone else do the dirty work for him because Lenny Friel was no thug. He was a legitimate business man. A solid, tax-paying, citizen. He was an employer, a pillar of the goddamn community. Sure, wasn't he having the streets cleaned up at this very moment?

A face appeared over his shoulder. Friel turned around.

"Hello," he tried smiling at his daughter, but the muscles in his face didn't work that way.

She rolled her eyes before walking away, a bottle of Innocent fruit smoothie in her hand. He wondered how much she'd overheard and if it mattered. She'd seen and heard enough while she was growing up to put the pieces together... if she wanted to. Not that there would be anything left to put together if he didn't bring this Boyle business to a sharp end.

Friel would get the diamonds and then Boyle would pay the real price of crossing him. An example had to be set, and to make the point clearly, the example would be brutal.

Boyle would have to die, and he'd have to die bad.

Chapter 25

Killian watched Jenny leave her flat again. Earlier he'd watched her leave for her morning run and was watching still when she returned. He hadn't followed her then, there was no need – he knew her routine – but he followed her now. She was off to university, bag slung over her shoulder, holding her head high, walking with a confident step. She looked happy. Well why wouldn't she? The girl was in love after all.

It amused him how she had fallen for him. He'd had other routes he could have taken otherwise, but this road was all the easier, all the sweeter. Like one of the Greek Gods, he had watched over her, anticipating her moves, manipulating her, testing her with tribulations, rewarding her with gifts. He was going to miss watching her when it was over.

No, that was a lie. It was the sensation of omnipotent power he was going to miss.

Pity he had to bring it to a head so quickly. He'd enjoyed playing it out slowly, gently luring her in, but Friel had told him to step it up and step it up he would. By the time he was finished with her, Boyle would be begging Friel to take the diamonds.

He walked behind her for a while, catching up and dropping back as the mood took him. Within touching distance one minute, letting her stride ahead the next. He savoured the knowledge that he was on her like her own shadow and she didn't know a thing about it.

He'd make a great Private Eye, or better still an assassin. Killian imagined a hypodermic in his hand as he closed in on her. It would be so simple to slide the needle into her as he passed, pressing the plunger neatly, efficiently, before losing himself once again in the morning throng.

Instead he jogged the last few paces to make it look as though he'd been trying to catch up and put a hand on her arm. She turned around with that startled look she gave every single time. It was hysterical. She worked really hard at putting on the confident air, yet it crumbled so easily. Poor little fragile Jenny.

The startled expression gave way to a smile. Expressions of delight poured forth from her lips as her hand fluttered around her heart indicating the fright he had given her. He kissed her lightly on the lips, standing close as he did so. She leaned into him.

"I missed you at the flat," he said. "I hoped I'd catch up with you – I've got you something."

He took a phone from his pocket.

"For me?"

"It's only a cheapo pay as you go, but I thought it would do until you got sorted with something better. At least this way we can keep in touch. Look, my number is already on it."

"Thank you, that is so thoughtful."

She kissed him, he kissed her back. Right there on the street, love's young dream. See how easy it was to please her? One cheapo phone and she was falling into his arms, but hey – it's the thought that counts, right?

Killian checked his watch. "I can walk with you for a bit if you like?"

"Are you sure you have time?"

He assured her he did, though he had rather less of it than he'd have liked. They held hands as they walked, their bodies close, a physical declaration of unity.

"How long do you think it takes to get to know someone?" she asked.

"I don't know, an eternity, maybe never… how well do we ever know anyone? On the other hand," he slowed their pace and looked into her eyes, "sometimes you meet someone and wham bam, it's like you've known them forever. You just get each other, you know?"

Ah, the smile on her face, the light and warmth of a thousand candles.

"Yes," she said. "I know."

"Why do you ask?"

Jenny shrugged. "It was just something Kaz – my flatmate – said last night after you'd gone."

"Yeah?" Alarm bells ringing, "what did she say?"

"That I didn't know anything about you, that you'd turned up out of the blue... It's not even true, you didn't turn up out of the blue – you're not just some random, we met at The Classic. It's like meeting anyone you've got a shared interest with."

"*Random?* Is that what she called me?"

"Yeah, that was another time."

"Sounds like she got to you a bit."

"It was the way that she said it. To be honest, I didn't realise she could be so bitchy."

"You know what? It sounds like she's trying to be a good friend. She's looking out for you, that's all."

"You think?"

"I think," he said. "Definitely."

"Yeah, maybe."

"So, how did it end up between you?" he asked.

"Not good," Jenny admitted. "I, er... slammed the door and went to my room."

Killian laughed, though just a little, calculating the right amount to make her laugh at herself, make her see the foolishness of her ways. To make her open up and tell him everything he needed to know.

"So, you went off in a huff?"

She rolled her eyes and laughed a little in return. "Yeah... I suppose I did. Stupid, huh?"

"Not really," toning down the smiles, turning up the empathy. "You were upset, but you know, like I said – she was being a friend. So how was it left, did you make up this morning?"

Jenny shook her head, the definition of rueful writ across her face. "No, didn't see her. She doesn't have a class until later on Fridays... I'll maybe see her at lunchtime."

Is that right?

"Yeah, you can make up then." Killian checked his phone. "Oh hell. Listen, Jenny – I'm gonna have to shoot right now, but I don't suppose…" He bade a twinkle to his eyes as he looked into hers.

"Don't suppose…?" The corners of her mouth twitching, eyes glittering with anticipation as she waited to hear what was coming next.

"I'm free from about two o'clock today – how about you…?"

Chapter 26

Boyle was sure he'd had worse nights, but he was struggling to remember when. The night he'd spent in a bus station in Birmingham had been pretty shit, but he hadn't had to put up with Elmer's snoring then, and though it had been cold, the Midlands chill was nought compared to the frost he was getting from Stella. He'd faced Elmer off for the sofa and won, but after the contortions he'd been in all night to make himself fit into it, he was wondering if Elmer had been practising the dark art of negative psychology on him. Maybe he wasn't as stupid as he looked. Or maybe he was used to sleeping on floors.

Elmer was awake but he was still on the floor, doing about 500,000 press-ups or so.

"Hey Elmer," Boyle's voice rasped. He was rolled up in the spare duvet he'd found in the wardrobe, his legs all kinked up.

Elmer halted mid press-up and looked at Boyle. "What?"

Boyle peered at him through one eye, the other was pressed into a cushion. Elmer had moved the coffee table out of the way and was exercising an arm's length away from him. Nothing hung loose, he was all muscles and tendons.

"Where do you live?" Boyle asked.

"Edinburgh."

"You stay with anyone?"

"Got my own place. Anything else?"

"Nah, carry on," Boyle said.

Elmer carried on while Boyle sat up and rubbed his face. He had cushion crush and more than a pang of envy. The facts were plain as Elmer's six pack – Boyle had failed at life. Even a lunk like Elmer had a place. What did Boyle have to show for his miserable existence? The imprint of creased fabric on his face and a big mess on his hands. He could call himself a drifter, but apart from making him sound like a wanker, it wasn't even true. He wasn't drifting, he was all snagged up in this mess.

What he fancied doing was cutting himself free and drifting on, and maybe he would have done... if it wasn't for Jenny. Another pang. This one tasted a lot like guilt. He hadn't been thinking enough about Jenny, it had been Stella, Stella, Stella, all the way.

He glanced through to the bedroom. The bed was made up, no sign of her.

"Where is she?" Boyle asked.

Elmer finished his routine and stood up in front of Boyle, his boxer-clad groin at a level with Boyle's face.

"Gone to get breakfast," Elmer said.

"Move out of the way, will you?"

"Whatever, Charlie."

Elmer moved. Boyle got up and went to the bathroom. He took off the clothes he'd slept in, had a shower then put them back on again. He'd left his bag in Marilyn's car. Marilyn... he looked at himself in the mirror as her name flitted through his mind. He could barely picture her face. She was already fading from his memory, leaving nothing behind but faint impressions of too much make-up around the eyes, skin as pale as moonlight, and the smell of liberally applied Chanel No.5. She was a country he'd pillaged, taking the best, leaving the rest, with nary a backward glance. She'd get over it.

Stella was there when he emerged, sitting in the armchair talking quietly to Elmer who was taking up more than his fair share of the sofa. She glanced at Boyle and looked away. Permafrost. He looked at Elmer. Elmer shrugged.

"Coffee and bacon rolls," he said.

Boyle squeezed in beside him. The coffee table was back in place, a cardboard carrying tray on it. There was one paper cup left in the tray. Boyle took it out and prised off the lid. The rich aroma of freshly brewed coffee perked him up. Small pleasures – he had to take them where he could get them. He took a couple of tongue-scorching sips before picking up one of the white paper bags. The first bacon roll went down without touching the sides so he helped himself to another. He caught Stella staring at him with a look of disgust and wiped the grease and flour from his face with a napkin.

"Man's got to eat," Elmer said to his sister.

She looked away, staring into nothing. She had on the same cashmere sweater as the night before and a pair of jeans. She looked good in them, but then Stella looked good in everything.

Boyle wiped his hands on a fresh napkin, then balled it up and tossed it onto the table with the rest of the breakfast debris.

"We going?" he asked.

Stella and Elmer exchanged glances. Boyle rolled his eyes.

"Will someone tell me what's going on?"

Elmer looked at Stella then at Boyle. "We can't go until this afternoon."

"Are you two at it? Why the hell not?" Boyle asked. He looked from one to the other, trying to get a handle on the situation, wondering if they were giving him the run around, but all he got in return was a pair of blank faces.

"Because there won't be anyone there," Stella said.

"All the better," Boyle said. "We go in, get the diamonds and leave and no one is any the wiser."

"I don't have a key," Stella said.

"*You what?* Oh please tell me this isn't true?"

"It's true," Elmer nodded his head.

"Well why did you leave them there in the first place?"

"She told you last night," Elmer said, "it was the safest place she could think of."

"Do you speak for her now?"

Stella slid him a sidewise look while Elmer did his blank stare. Boyle couldn't figure if Elmer really was as dumb as he looked or if the whole dumbass lunk persona was an act, nothing but a big old confidence trick. He ran his hands over his face. "Oh man," he said, "this just gets better and better. Look, tell you what we'll do – you drive me up there, tell me exactly where they are and I'll break in and get them."

"You can't do that," Stella said.

"Thanks for sparing me the words – so why not? It'll be easy peasy, in-out, wham-bam, thank you ma'am."

"You just can't… someone is bound to see you. There are neighbours and he gets visitors all the time. Look, it's only another couple of hours. Just wait and you'll get your precious diamonds."

"Those *precious diamonds* as you put it, Stella baby, are going to save my *precious daughter.*"

"Oh yeah," Elmer said, "Your daughter. I forgot about her. What's her name again?"

"Her name is Jenny."

Chapter 27

Killian glanced at the screen, Friel again. The man had called him last night for the purpose of delivering a stream of vitriol, wrath and fear directly into Killian's auditory canal. The fear being Friel's own, unintentionally conveyed as he ranted. Killian sucked in a deep breath, preparing himself for another unhinged tirade as he answered the call.

"Yes, I'm on it… yes, today…" *Yes, yes, yes, fuckity, yessity, yes, yes.*

When the man was done venting, Killian put the phone back in his pocket. Friel was losing it. A little bit of pressure and he was coming apart at the seams. Problem with Lenny Friel was he'd gone unchallenged for too long. He'd become complacent, all cosied down in the niche he'd carved out for himself, cushioned by fat, lazy bastards like Bobby Big Cheeks and Spanish Tony. Once upon a time in Govan they might have been hard men but when was the last time either of them had got their hands mucky never mind dirty?

Friel had made the mistake of thinking that what he had was his by divine right, that he was untouchable. He was old school, old back to the dawn of time, relying on a reputation as aged as Methuselah. Bobby and Tony were dinosaurs. They hadn't cottoned on that there was a new breed in town.

A betting man might have put money on Friel's days of wine and roses coming to an end. There was probably a book running on it right now, but no matter the odds, Killian's money was staying in his pocket.

Friel had the fear alright. It wasn't just the irrational, spit-launching tirades down the phone that gave him away - Killian could smell it on him. But the thing Killian found interesting about fear was its unpredictable effects. What may make one man quake, lending a tremble to his hand, may induce another to piss his pants or soil himself, but may yet have a more profound effect on a third, filling him with a nothing-to-lose frenzy, rendering him volatile and dangerous. It paid to be cautious around such a person.

Without benefit of a crystal ball, Killian had no idea how this situation was going to play out, but for sure when it came to Lenny Friel, he planned on exercising extreme caution. Friel's edge may have been dulled, but it would be a foolish man who raised swords against him.

And what of good friend, Kaz? She had about her the demeanour of one who had never been properly acquainted with fear. She could talk about it in abstract terms, of that he was sure. The woman could talk for Scotland on all manner of subjects, rabbiting forth with her unqualified opinions on unsuitable suitors and suchlike, but how would she react when life took a chunk out of her arse? What then, Ms High and Mighty? A little dribbling in the panties, mayhap, but he couldn't see her actually pissing herself. She'd gain control of her bladder quickly enough, but what of her tongue? Would she tighten her lips, pulling them bloodless and taut around a silent mouth, or go running to fair Jenny, loosening them in her ear, giving them a workout of Olympian proportions? Risky, risky, which way would the cat jump?

Perhaps this feline required to be flayed in a different style.

It was past ten when she emerged from the flat. She was tall, five ten anyway, one of those people who owned their own space. She didn't have to feign confidence, life was a gift to this one.

Killian followed her along the street, watching for an opportunity to introduce a chance encounter. It came when she entered the local independent coffee shop. He followed her in, taking his place behind her in the queue, not noticing her until she paid for her order and turned, latte in hand, and then perchance, his gaze grazed hers. In a beautifully executed transition he raised his eyebrows in surprised recognition. She, caught on the back foot, allowed a momentary sliver of unconscious dislike to mar her expression before the blank mask of indifferent politeness came crashing down like a portcullis on her visage.

"Hi," he said, "Kaz, isn't it?"

She nodded.

"Michael – Jenny's-"

"I know who you are."

"Americano, please," he said to the barista. "Yeah," he smiled at Kaz, "of course you do. Listen, you couldn't wait up a second, just till I get my coffee?"

"I don't know, I-" She looked away.

The smile inside him broadened as he watched her squirm. The urge within her to refuse him was strong, but it was straining against the even more powerful and deeply ingrained compulsion to be polite and play by the rules of convention.

"I'll just be a sec."

He paid for his coffee and turned to her. "Got a minute?" He nodded at the counter by the window where customers could stand and drink their coffee as they watched the world pass by.

"I don't know I-"

"Please? It will only take a moment, otherwise I'll have to stalk you until you listen." His tone just-joking light, his smile warm, gaze sincere.

She half-smiled, un-smiled and shruggy-smiled. To walk out on him now would be difficult, more difficult than staying.

"I can't stay for long."

"It won't take long, I promise." He flashed a modest trust-me smile.

She nodded though she didn't want to, and walked to the counter ahead of him. He stood beside her, close enough to quietly converse but careful not to encroach on her personal space. He wanted defences down, not up. She looked at him, inviting him to start the conversation.

"Er, I'm not sure quite where to start with this," he looked down and rubbed the back of his neck before glancing up to catch her gaze. He flashed an embarrassed smile. The corners of her mouth softened. "Look, I'll come right out and say it – I caught the look you threw me last night… I have to tell you, Kaz, I've seen some dirty looks in my time, but that was a belter." She opened her mouth to speak but he hushed her with a raised palm. "No, please, now that I've started, you've got to let me get this out. Look, I understand where you're coming from. Jenny was upset – it looked like I'd upset her… well, I had upset her, but it was unintentional. I can see it from your point of view – I'm this guy who appears out of nowhere, she doesn't know me, you guys – her good friends – don't know me – I get it, I could be anybody, right?"

A flush arose in Kaz's face as her own words fluttered towards her and came home to roost. She shrugged, nodded.

"It's okay," he said, "I understand, there are a lot of crazy people out there – you're just looking out for your friend – for Jenny." He paused for a moment, just long enough to let an expression of bliss drift across his face at the mention of her name. "The truth is, Kaz," heartfelt words delivered with a direct look in the eye, "I'm as surprised at all of this as you. Meeting Jenny…" looking down, embarrassed at revealing his inner pink, "…has changed my life."

A moment passed, then two. *Tick tock.*

"Hey," Kaz reached out to him, touching him on the arm. Slam dunk, connection made. "It's okay," she said. "I get it – you two are mad for each other."

Killian looked up and into her face.

"Yeah, we are… I'd never do anything to hurt her. I need you to know that."

"You'd better not."

They laughed at the same time, though not necessarily at the same thing.

She left, apologising for having to run. He apologised back for taking up her time. She called him Michael and told him she was glad he had – it was good running into each other like that.

It surely was, he thought as he watched her leave the shop, turning briefly to give him a small wave as she did so. He waved back at his new Best Friend Forever. They were bosom buddies. Even now she'd be planning on introducing him to her boyfriend, telling him what a great guy Michael Killian was, and how sweet it was that he was so nuts about Jenny, and she about him and how they should all hang out together. Saturday night double dates, bowls of popcorn, bottles of beer, laughter, friendship, creating memories. Good times, people, good times.

Though outwardly he gave nothing away, Killian's inside smile was wide. The situation was resolved. He needed a clean set-up, and he had one. Now there was little to nil chance of Kaz kicking up a fuss when Jenny disappeared. She would have no sinister thoughts in her head about Jenny going off with her new boyfriend… her lovely, charming and ever so sincere boyfriend. The pair of them all loved-up together. Sweet was what it was.

Sweet indeed. Killian checked his watch. The talking time was done. Now it was the time for doing.

Chapter 28

"What's that?" Friel asked.

His daughter rolled her eyes and sighed. "You know what it is."

"Been scraped off the bottom of a budgie's cage is what it is." Friel pushed the bowl of granola aside. "How's a man supposed to function with that inside him? I could murder a bacon roll. Where's your mother anyway?"

He looked around as if expecting Debs to materialise on command.

"Out."

"Out? The woman's never in. Where the hell is she now?"

"Duh - work?"

Friel bristled at the village-idiot look his daughter gave him.

"At this time?"

He fought down the urge to slap the sarcastic expression off her face as she raised a practiced eyebrow, glancing instead at the kitchen clock. He was surprised to see that it had gone half nine. His wife was where she was supposed to be, floating around one of her salons, yakking and drinking coffee and buttering up her clientele. He on the other hand had slept late and felt like he was a battery down. Everything was out of kilter, including the fact that his daughter was here at all.

"How are you not at school?"

"Study period."

Every word a prisoner. She picked up a piece of jam-laden toast with her iPod-free hand and drifted off in the direction of her room, eyes on the screen, Friel relegated to background scenery. He had ceased to exist.

He felt like grabbing her by the shoulders and giving her a bloody good shake. He wanted to scream in her face and scare the attitude right out of her. He wanted to wake her up from her bloody catatonic state, to make her realise how lucky she was to lead the life she did. He wanted her to be grateful for everything he'd done, to show some appreciation, or at the very least just acknowledge his existence once in a while.

Her bedroom door slammed as she kicked it closed behind her. Friel's gaze fell on the bowl of cereal Debs had left out for him. He swept it off the counter. As if to spite him, the bowl bounced and rolled instead of shattering. He stared at the scattered oats, nuts and dried fruit. Rabbit food. The kind of shite he imagined Michael Killian eating. Load of my-body-is-a-temple bollocks.

Michael was full of it and then some, but it was time he came up with the goods. He needed reminding about that.

Friel called him, pacing up and down as he snarled into the phone, granola grinding underfoot.

Michael gave him all the right answers, made all the right noises - *yes, today...yes, yes, yes* - but his knowing words did not sate Friel. He hung up, the rage still expanding within him. He needed something – or someone - he could get stuck into. He narrowed his eyes, the lines running from them deep and dark.

Charlie Boyle was at the root of this. Friel took the other phone from his pocket. Jenny's phone. Boyle - *Charlie Boyle* - the sound of the name in his head was enough to splinter Friel's teeth.

He called. Boyle answered.

Jenny?

The hope in Boyle's voice gave Friel a kick. "No not Jenny. Sorry to disappoint."

Where is she? Is she alright?

"Relax, she's fine... for now."

What do you want?

"I want my diamonds."

You'll get them.

"When, Charlie? When am I going to get them?"

Today – tonight-

"Well what is it then, today or tonight? It's a simple

enough question."

Boyle tried to speak, but Friel bulldozed right through him, battering Boyle with a relentless barrage of needling wind-ups.

"What is it with you, anyway, Boyle? Is your head not screwed on right? Can you do up your own buttons yet? Does your maw still wipe your arse for you?"

Friel kicked the cereal bowl aside. Finally, he was getting some satisfaction.

"No, wait a minute... it's something else, isn't it? You wouldn't be giving me the run-around, Charlie? That's it, isn't it – you're taking the piss, aren't you Charlie? You don't want to do that, seriously – you don't."

I'm not – I swear. Tonight, definitely tonight – where do you want me to bring them?

Friel shook his head. "Charlie, Charlie – just when I thought we were getting somewhere. That's not the way this game is played. You don't ask me – you don't get to ask me anything. I tell you - you understand?"

A pause before Boyle answered.

I understand.

"Good boy, Charlie. Now you're catching on." Friel's lips twisted and smirked at the laden silence emanating from the other end of the call. Boyle was on the back foot, but Friel wanted more, much more.

"You're a quick study, Charlie, but maybe not quick enough."

Another pause before Boyle's hesitant response.

What do you mean?

"What I mean is... I don't think you have grasped the gravity of your – of Jenny's - situation. I feel – Charlie – that you suffer from a lack of empathy – particularly when it comes to your lovely daughter. The impression you have given me, Charlie, is that I could tie her in a sack with a half dozen bricks and throw her in the Clyde and you, my friend, would not give a shit."

That's not true.

"You say that, but do you mean it? Even for an ex-copper, you are not a right person. You are a bit off, Charlie, know what I mean? I just want to know if you care about Jenny. Well do you, Charlie? Do you care? Do you really care? Deep within you, do you care?"

I care, I care – I swear. Please... don't hurt her.

The rising panic in Boyle's voice, the way it snarled up his vocal chords, was as a heavenly choir to Friel's ears.

"You messed with the wrong man, Charlie. You understand? When you took those diamonds you messed with the wrong man."

I'm sorry, I didn't know about Sammy's debt – please, don't hurt her.

Friel's smirk broke into a broad grin. Boyle's pleading pleased him. There was even a hint of a sob in his voice. Oh yes. This was breakfast, this was something he could sink his teeth into.

"I'm afraid it's too late for that, Charlie."

He hung up, cutting Boyle off mid-plea.

He felt better now. He would stop off at Paddy's van on the way to the yard, treat himself to a big fat bacon roll. Maybe get Paddy to sling on a slice of black pudding while he was at it. He was just about tasting it when a sudden gleam caught his gaze. He turned his head. His daughter was staring at him, halogen lights glinting on her iPod screen.

"Sweetheart!" Friel smiled. His smile, containing residual pleasure from his call to Boyle along with some warmth from the thought of the bacon roll he would soon be consuming, was heartfelt.

"I didn't see you come in. Have you been there long?"

"Long enough."

He searched her face for signs of disquiet or disgust. On finding none, he looked longer and deeper. His daughter continued to hold his gaze, one eyebrow slightly raised. He supposed by now that she had seen and heard enough, picking up morsels here, titbits there, to piece together a picture if she so chose. Debs chose not. Debs preferred to scatter the pieces to the wind and cast her gaze in other directions, a situation with which Lenny Friel had no argument, but the daughter was a different animal. The daughter looked directly at Friel and saw him for what he was. What's more, it appeared that she had little problem with the knowing.

"You should be at school," he said.

"Okay, dad." She smiled at him.

It had been a long time since she'd treated him with such warm courtesy. He watched as she walked away from him, long hair draping down her back, hips swinging, her movements effortlessly graceful. They had created a monster. A beautiful monster.

Friel smiled.

Better the predator than the prey.

Chapter 29

Her name is Jenny.

Yeah, right. Keep reminding yourself, Charlie, and maybe it will stick. He stared at Stella but she'd sent him to a virtual gulag and was making like he didn't exist. *She* was the real reason he was here. She'd been the reason ever since he first laid eyes on her. She was like a sickness he couldn't shake. Sending the shivers down his nerve ends while she burned him up inside.

He should cut out this sickness called Stella and cast it from him. He'd tried before, but this time he'd do it for real. He'd take a scalpel to himself then stitch up the wound and walk away without looking back, just like before… only this time he'd cut deep and sure and he really would walk away instead of circling around the same old territory, kidding himself on that he wasn't on the sniff for a few scraps from her table. He'd go find a place he could start afresh. No more backstreet pubs and lonely landladies… and no more Stella. He would go legit. Pick himself up a nice, normal job. Put in an honest day's work for an honest day's wage. Laughing at himself even as he formed the thought, because that was the way it worked for sure. Besides, there was the Jenny situation to consider, after all that's why he was here…

Boyle sneered at himself. He'd been spot-on earlier. He really had failed at life. Failed husband, failed copper, failed father. The friends he'd accumulated over a lifetime he could count on the fingers of one hand and he'd failed them as well, though when it came to Macallister *fail* hardly covered it.

He'd taken a one-way trip to Loathsome Town and was treating himself to a wallow in the muddy waters of self-pity when his phone rang.

He looked at the screen. "Jenny?" he answered. Voice full of hope that really, Jenny was fine. It had been a mix-up, or a prank gone wrong. Maybe Jenny's idea of punishing him for being such an arse of a father. That's okay, he didn't blame her. He deserved that and more, but now that she'd had her fun maybe it would be better for all concerned if he disappeared over the horizon.

These thoughts and more tumbled and bounced through his head in the brief time it took for him to look at the screen and speak her name, but it wasn't Jenny – it was *him*. Lenny Friel. Glasgow accent, grit in the throat, on a fishing expedition and he had Boyle on his hook. Boyle was going nowhere. The voice drilled into him, draining the colour from his face, turning his muscles to soup, his spine to a column of melting ice, until he was nothing but a heap of wet mush held together by skin.

The sack of mush that once had been a man called Boyle listened and answered and pleaded. *Please, don't hurt her*, still begging as the call went dead in his hand.

He stood up on weak legs, his gut wriggling and writhing like a sack of worms, his insides ready to spew forth. Stella and Elmer stared at him, mouths hanging open, dark pupils of their eyes consuming him as he lumbered to the bathroom.

The taste of coffee was sour and stale in his mouth but nothing came up. He leaned over the wash hand basin, resting the top of his head against the mirror, staring down into the plug-hole. Still with his head against the mirror, he turned on the cold tap. Turned it on full so that the water bounced and swirled around the sink, spraying him before it whirled down the dark hole into the network of pipes leading to the sewer.

He knocked his head against the glass, hard enough to hurt, hard enough to make him feel, but not hard enough to break. He couldn't break, not the mirror, not himself, not if he was to be of any use to his daughter.

He leaned off the mirror and sluiced his face before turning off the tap. When he took the drying towel from his face Elmer was standing before him.

"We'll help you get her back, buddy."

"We?" Boyle asked.

"Yeah, me and Stella. We'll help you, buddy."

Boyle felt so grateful he could weep. It wasn't like him, neither the overwhelming sense of gratitude nor the urge to sob. It was as though somewhere along the broken line of his life he had lost every part of him that made him himself. Maybe that was a good thing.

He walked through to the sitting room, propelling himself by placing one foot in front of the other, just like that. Amazed that he could do it without thinking, especially as his mind now felt some distance from his body. Stella was standing by the window, looking at the river.

"You mean it?" he asked, wondering who it was doing the asking and how come they were able to make the words come out of his mouth.

She nodded. "Yes, Charlie. I mean it." He made a move, meaning to fall into her arms, find some solace there, but she turned away from him. "No," she told him. "We'll get the diamonds, and you can have them. Use them to get your daughter back. But then we are done."

He backed off. "Okay Stella, if that's the way you want it."

"That's the way it has to be, Charlie."

She walked away from him then, and though she didn't go far, only through to the bedroom where she picked things up and moved them around, he felt lost and alone and he did not know who he was or what he meant.

Chapter 30

It was a one-off. She was serious about her studies, but all work and no play made Jenny a dull little beast. Besides, skipping one lousy lecture wasn't going to bring her degree crumbling down around her ears.

Nevertheless, she was ever so slightly terrified of the not turning up which brought her to the conclusion that she wasn't one of life's natural rule-breakers. Which, given the lightness of her step and the euphoric fizz of anticipation bubbling up inside her, led her to next think that perhaps she should break out of her comfort zone a little more often.

It wasn't as if she was cutting the lecture for trivial matters – what could be less trivial than love? Spell it out, girl – L.O.V.E. Four little letters, one big emotion, not to mention those three little letters S.E.X. First time for love, first time for sex, first time for missing a lecture. It was a day of firsts.

The popping candy on the cake was the gushing apology she'd received when Kaz had sought her out at lunch to tell her how wrong she'd been about Michael. But how, why, Jenny had asked. Turned out they had run into each other at Caffeine Quirks. It was funny – he had been in such a rush. Probably needed a caffeine injection to see him on his way.

Kaz, in the wrong – who'd a thunk it? Jenny grinned wide and felt the joy deep. She and Michael were going to spend the rest of the day – and night – together. Maybe the whole weekend.

I know it's soon, Jenny, but it's how I feel. I want to be with you.
And I want to be with you too, Michael.
Are you sure I'm not rushing you?
I'm sure.

She was back in the flat, had packed herself an overnight bag, and now she was waiting for Michael. The weekend would start when he picked her up.

She had never thought of herself as a romantic, but now her head was filled with the movies she had watched alone at The Classic. Bette Davis telling Paul Henreid not to ask for the moon when they had the stars, and now here she was - Jenny Boyle with Michael laying the stars, the moon and all the heavenly bodies before her.

The ping of an incoming text alerted her to his imminent arrival. She watched from the window for his car, waving when he arrived to let him know she'd seen him, and then she was out and down the stairs and he was waiting for her, all smiles, and full of the happiness and the joy of seeing her.

As they drove from the West End to the City Centre, she looked at the town as if she had never seen it before, everything new and fresh and exciting. Gothic towers reaching into gunmetal skies, lives stacked and squared in red sandstone buildings, the sweep of elegant Georgian terraces with their tall, precise windows and neat railings like a scene from the set of *Oliver!* New buildings of steel, chrome and glass, wirings and workings on display, and everywhere people, milling, rushing, dawdling, gawping, breathing, crying, lying and how many of them in love? How many of them feeling as unutterably alive as she did?

"I love this city," Michael said. He was so totally in tune with her.

"Me too – and I never realised how much, until now."

The look on his face as he returned her smile told her that he got it. He was in this moment with her, getting it, understanding it, feeling it. What were the chances, she wondered, that in a city with a population of nearly 600,000 that the two of them should meet?

"Do you think it's true," she asked, "that there is someone for everyone?"

"I do now," he said.

He parked in a private underground carpark and they rode the elevator to the sixth floor. The interior of the lift was all smoked glass and polished surfaces. Swish was the word that came into her mind, apt though it was she could not recall using it before. Another first.

Anticipation fluttered within her like a creature alive in its own right as he unlocked the door to his flat. It was not only the thought of being with him – of doing *it* – that had her all a quiver, it was this, the very entering of his domain. Seeing where he lived, how he arranged his life, the personal details and quirks of it.

The immediate impression was of space. A generous hall led to a large open-plan living area incorporating the kitchen. There were none of the strewn clothes, scattered books or abandoned shoes she become accustomed to on flat-sharing with Andrea. Kaz was tidier, Michael tidier still. This much she had expected, deducing from his dress and the way he presented himself that he was an orderly type with an eye for detail. The lines of the room were clean, the furniture – what there was of it – modern and stylish. This too came as no surprise. What did take her aback was the absoluteness of it.

"Wow, you're a real minimalist," she said, adding - when he glanced at her, "I just mean, it's so… clutter-free."

He looked around as though noticing the room for the first time. "You should see the cupboards," he said. "Always buy a place with plenty of storage."

Now that Michael was pointing it out, Jenny realised a section of one wall was made of discreet, built-in closets and drawers.

"Neat," she said.

"Not inside they aren't. I'd show you, but I'm too embarrassed."

She laughed. "That's okay," she said. "You should see the mess under my bed."

He took her jacket and hung it beside his own in one of the closets then went to the fridge and took out a bottle of champagne, "I know it's early, but…"

"Why not?"

He took two champagne flutes from a cupboard and opened the bottle.

"That's not the first time you've done that," she said as he brought her a filled glass.

"No, but I've never enjoyed doing it quite so much

before. To us."

"To us," she echoed.

They stood by the kitchen island, making small talk as they sipped champagne. The conversation flowing from their lips meant nothing, it was all in the eyes - in his eyes. Jenny gazed into them, entranced, barely aware of their bodies moving closer together until they were touching. He took the glass from her hand and sat it on the counter beside his. When he kissed her she felt as though she was melting into him, the two of them becoming one.

Lost in his embrace, she barely noticed as they moved to the bedroom. The curtains were already drawn, the room lit by the soft glow of hidden light.

"Are you sure?" he asked.

"Yes," she replied, her voice barely a whisper.

They undressed slowly. She looked away when she got down to her bra, until he touched her lightly under the chin and tilted her face towards his.

"You are beautiful," he said.

"I feel beautiful when I'm with you."

She felt she ought to be embarrassed by her immodest declaration, but here, now, with him, she did feel beautiful and with that realisation her confidence grew and so Jenny removed her remaining clothing and stood before him naked, unblushing, and Michael too stripped off and it all felt so very natural. She was beautiful, he was beautiful, they were two beautiful people together, full of warmth and desire and a longing to touch and hold and make love. And make love they did.

There was a moment when first he entered her that she felt pain – no, not pain, an unsettling more like at the strangeness of it – and then came the pleasure as she relaxed and introduced her own beats to his rhythm until the two of them were moving as one. Being suddenly aware of this, there came into her mind the line from Othello about making the beast with two backs, only they were not a beast, they were a beautiful creature, naked and writhing and moaning, pheromones singing, hearts pounding as the fibres of the creature's muscles contracted and relaxed, bunching and loosening until the final release, and with a cry there was nothing more to do but fall back into two separate entities, their bodies slick with sweat. Except they were not quite separate. Contact continued where their arms touched and also along the stretch of their legs.

Jenny's head rested on a king size pillow stuffed with down and encased in crisp, white, Egyptian cotton with a thread count in the stratosphere. So generous, so full of pillowness that it gave the impression of never having had a head laid on it before. She wondered if it was all new – the sheets, the duvet, the pillows, perhaps even the bed and all of it, all of this newness, was for her.

He turned to her and traced a finger on her cheek.

"Are you okay?" he asked.

She smiled and told him yes.

"I want to remember this moment forever," he said.

"Me too."

She'd listened to stories, told over too-sweet cocktails and glasses of wine, of terrible first times, hoots of laughter spiralling over embarrassing anecdotes, each teller trying to outdo the last in terms of awkwardness and clumsiness and the sheer and utter hellishness of the experience, but none of that was for Jenny. Her first experience of sex had been a revelation. She had been blind but now she could see.

"What are you smiling at?" he asked.

"Nothing much, I'm just happy."

He twiddled with her hair for a while, curling it around his fingers, smiling as he did so, before saying, "I know."

He got out of bed and raked around in his clothes.

"What do you know?" she asked.

She sat up, making sure her modesty was preserved by the duvet as she watched him.

He held up his phone.

"No," she said, a flush rising.

He sat on the edge of the bed. "Please," stroking her face

again, "we should preserve the moment."

She hesitated, not wanting to spoil the mood by refusing him.

"Please," he said again, a teasing smile on his face, "you look so beautiful."

"I bet I don't."

He placed a quieting hand over hers as she fussed with her hair.

"Seriously, Jenny – you look amazing." He waggled his phone. "Please, just one… please, for me?"

"Oh go on then – but just the one."

She checked that the duvet was covering everything from her armpits down and smiled as he took the photograph. Strange how exposed she felt though only her arms and shoulders were on display. Stranger yet was the tingle of excitement it gave her. That she was pretty was a fact akin to the sky being blue, grass green and fairy tales having happy endings, but suddenly Jenny felt more than pretty – a label she considered hollow at any rate – now she felt beautiful, and not only beautiful, but desirable. The idea excited her, aroused her even, and so when Michael suggested taking another picture, she agreed, and when he teased down the top of the duvet to take a third she allowed him to do so. And thus it went on, until it wasn't Michael who was drawing the cotton aside, but Jenny.

Exposing her breasts was disinhibiting, it was only skin, only flesh after all. Michael made appreciative sounds as she pouted and posed, enticing her to go a little further, to extend the boundaries, break down the artificial restraints imposed by society.

"Let yourself go, Jenny."

The duvet slid off the bed leaving Jenny – by accident or design – fully exposed to the lens. She laughed because Michael was laughing and as they had already been laughing it seemed like the thing to do. And when he placed a hand on her knee and smoothed his palm down the inside of her thigh thus parting her legs, she allowed him to do so.

Legs spread, her vulva displayed, he encouraged her to part her labia, exposing all that she had for his lens. This she did, but even as she displayed herself she realised that the game had gone too far. At some point between the duvet slithering to the floor and the image taken of her vagina, a boundary had been crossed.

Jenny closed her legs and reached for the duvet, pulling it over herself. Covered to her chin, she glanced at Michael, wary of his reaction in case he mocked her for being a prude. It had been so magical, so wonderful up to that indefinable point that she could not bear for the atmosphere to sour between them, but Michael seemed unperturbed. He pulled on his jeans and slipped his phone into his pocket, looking at her and talking to her as if nothing in particular had occurred. He told her he was hungry. Thought that she must be too. There was pizza in the fridge.

"Why don't you jump in the shower, I'll put the pizza in the oven and join you."

"Okay," she said.

Her voice felt small and stupid, the moment of feeling beautiful and desirable and of radiating sensuality having passed. Michael left the bedroom showing no sign of being disconcerted in any way. Jenny stared at the space he had previously occupied, his place taken by air and dust motes. As she stared she realised what had happened. Michael had carried on taking photographs until the moment she said stop and then he had simply stopped. There had been no quibble, no question, no attempt to persuade her to carry on. He respected her boundaries, pure and simple. The only person in this situation with their feathers all a-ruffled was little Jenny Wren.

Okay, all she had to do was say stop. End of story. And ask him to delete the photographs – some of them anyway. Maybe most of them. The lasts ones definitely. And then it would all be fine.

Head straightened, feathers smoothed, Jenny got out of bed and went to the en-suite shower room Michael suggested she use. The urge within her was to scurry, to hide her nakedness, if only from herself, but she forced herself to walk slowly, hips swinging, once again owning her bare flesh. Her confidence grew with each step and so by the time she reached the door she had regained some of that inner goddess feeling.

White, fluffy towels neatly stacked awaited within a shower room as neat and tidy and new looking as the rest of his place. The shower was a large walk-in. Products with smart labels were arranged on a shelf in the shower and beside the wash hand basin.

Jenny closed the door and quickly used the toilet before he came back. She needn't have worried - she'd been in the shower for several minutes before he joined her. Her face flushed when he opened the screen door and stood there naked taking a good long look at her nakedness. She blushed, the blush deepening as her embarrassment increased, catching her in a vicious circle of embarrassment feeding embarrassment.

She hated feeling so naïve, but if he noticed he wasn't letting on, besides, it wasn't her face his attention was on and given what was going on with him, he liked what he saw. Looking at his erect penis only increased the ferocity of the heat in her face and so she looked away from him altogether until his looking time was done and he got in beside her.

Suddenly his hands were all over her, hers all over his, his desire exciting her. He pushed her thighs apart with his leg and thrust himself inside her. She gasped at the abrupt intrusion, her back bruising against cold tiles as he thrust again and again and again. Water ran into her eyes and filled her mouth when she tried to tell him to… tell him what? To stop? Yes, she wanted him to stop. This wasn't what it was supposed to be like. They were not sharing – he was taking something from her. Taking, taking, taking-

Her hands beating on his back only encouraged him to thrust harder and deeper. She clawed at him, but her nails were short, his skin slick, and then he gasped and his body relaxed, his slack weight bearing down on her, crushing the breath from her lungs, leaving her unable to speak. No matter – she had no words. No cohesive thoughts, only a momentous feeling that she had made a mistake.

He finally leaned off her, smiling as he said, "I enjoyed that."

He pumped a handful of shower gel from the dispenser and turned his back on her as he lathered himself. "Do my back, will you."

Jenny obeyed. This confined space with its hard surfaces was no place for dissent.

"That's good," he said, the muscles in his back writhing under her hand.

He rinsed off quickly and got out of the shower telling her, as he tied a towel around his waist, that if she spent any longer in there she was going to prune up.

She turned off the water. He handed her a towel. Still in the shower cabinet, she wrapped it tightly around herself, tucking it under her arms. When she got out he manoeuvred her until she was staring at herself in the non-steam mirror as he loomed behind her.

"That was good," he said. "Really good." He kissed her on the shoulders and neck. "This is going to be an unforgettable weekend."

He turned then and walked out, all sinews and muscles and strength, leaving her weak and bruised and still staring at her reflection. Her hair hung about her face in damp, dark, straggles. She thought she knew him, but she didn't. She thought she knew herself, now she was doubting even that. When it came right down to it, she wasn't even entirely sure of where she was.

Slowly it dawned on her that neither did anyone else. No-one that was, but Michael.

Chapter 31

It was a half hour drive from Perth to the market town where daddy dearest abided. By all accounts the mother lived there too, though she had only been mentioned in passing. A bit-player in her own family. There was scenery en-route if you liked that kind of thing. Boyle didn't much care. He looked without seeing, staring through the windscreen from the front passenger seat. Stella was driving.

They were in Marilyn's car, information Boyle considered to be on a strictly need-to-know basis, and Stella did not need to know. What she didn't know couldn't hurt her. If only the same applied to Jenny.

She didn't know about the diamonds, or Stella, or Sammy Macallister but still the situation threatened her. Stupid expression in the first place – plenty of people were hurt by things they didn't know - but it wasn't half as stupid as the drivel Elmer was spouting in the back seat. Words flowed from his mouth, the meaning of them – if they had any in the first instance – passing Boyle by. Maybe the sound had purpose in its own right, filling what would otherwise have been a jaw clenching silence.

It was only mid-afternoon, but it had already been a long day, the morning stretching like an endless abyss as they waited for the minutes to tick by until, finally, they could leave.

Boyle hadn't entirely bought into Stella's reason for making them wait, but Elmer backed her up and wasn't for backing down. Boyle, being in no mood to tackle the big lunk, guessed another couple of hours wouldn't matter, which led him to wondering if anything mattered ever.

Elmer tried to cajole Boyle into a game of cards to pass the time but Boyle wasn't up for it. All he wanted to do was brood and twitch and work on the dark mood arising within him. Elmer played solitaire. Later, Elmer gave a running commentary as he flipped through the television channels, pausing a little longer when he came across a DNA result on the Jeremy Kyle Show. Later still, Elmer paced around the room, touching things, moving things. After that, Elmer stood by the window and gave another running commentary, this time on the traffic crossing the bridge.

Boyle tried to ignore him but it was like trying to block a persistent fly, the kind that floats around your head and no matter how many times you swat and flick at it, it keeps coming back, just hanging in the air, annoying the life out of you until you get to the stage where the only thing you can think about is the fly and how crazy it makes you feel.

Stella meanwhile, was unperturbed. Did that mean Boyle was perturbed? He'd never heard of anyone being called perturbed, but it was as good a label as any. Perturbed man watching unperturbed woman pack her bags.

"Where you gonna go, sis?" Elmer asked.

He was in the bedroom area, picking up items of clothing and handing them to Stella. It seemed to Boyle an intimate kind of scene. He told himself to cool it, that they were brother and sister. He told himself he didn't care, but he wasn't listening.

"I don't know," Stella said, "but I'm not coming back here."

"You can come to my place, you know that – stay as long as you like."

"I know – thank you, Elmer."

She stopped what she was doing to touch him on the arm and when she smiled at Elmer it was as if a light had come on inside her, but Boyle knew she was never planning on staying at his place. Stella knew it, and as Elmer was nowhere near as daft as he looked, Boyle guessed he knew it too.

"This is it," Stella said.

She turned off the road and parked in the drive of a heavy stone villa. Though smaller in scale, it had the look about it of a Victorian orphanage. The kind where laughter was rare and no matter how big the fire in the hearth, the chill persisted, frosting the windows on the inside. The trees surrounding it were mostly bare, stark branches reaching into the air like hands raised in horror.

"Nice," Boyle said.

"It comes with the job."

"What job?" Boyle asked, but Stella ignored him.

"You two wait here – it will be easier if I go alone."

"Sure, sis," Elmer said, an obedient pup.

Boyle said nothing. The last thing he wanted was an introduction to dear old Paw. Stella got out of the car and walked to the door. She could hold the light of a room, but as she approached the house it seemed to Boyle that she diminished like a guttering candle.

He shifted in his seat, his innards feeling like they were in the grasp of a tightening fist. It killed him to see her looking so vulnerable – it brought all the old feelings to the fore. He truly believed the day would come when he would be able to stop caring about her, but today was not that day.

"What job?" he repeated, seeking distraction.

"Thought you knew," Elmer said. "The old man's a minister."

"So you're the son of the manse?"

"Nah, I'm the bastard of the manse. Stella's the legit one, not that it did her much good."

"How so?"

Boyle caught a glimpse of another woman as the front door opened and Stella stepped inside. Small in stature, greying hair and a face that looked as though it was permanently worried, was all the impression he got before the door closed on them.

"He's a cold bastard of a man. Don't think he ever approved of her much more than he approved of me."

"If he's so cold, how come you exist?"

"You know, Charlie, that's a question I've often pondered myself. The old dear's dead and gone these last four years but when she was still on the go she was mostly tight-lipped on the subject of him... except that is when she got herself drammed up."

"Liked a drink, did she?"

"Rarely, Charlie, rarely – but when she tippled, she tippled hard. Mr Whyte and Mr Mackay were her companions and when she was with them her lips loosened and her tongue waggled. It was like she'd been holding back on all those words like water held behind a dam, and when that dam burst – Charlie, I'm telling you - those words, they came pouring and tumbling and gushing out all at once."

"So what did she say?"

"She said that he could turn on the charm, that his eyes could go from cold to warm and back again, just like that." Elmer snapped his fingers in illustration.

Like father like daughter, Boyle thought.

"He charmed her right into bed with his warm eyes and soothing words, and this he did on several occasions until he planted a seed that took. That's how she said it, Charlie, *until he planted a seed that took*. Well the seed took, and her belly began to swell and then his eyes grew cold and they never looked on her with warmth again. My mother…" Elmer's words faltered.

Sounded to Boyle like Elmer had himself been holding back a lot of words for a long time. Boyle continued staring at the manse as he waited for Elmer to gather himself. He was glad there was no danger of eye contact. Hearing the confession was one thing, but the sight of a man exposing his vulnerabilities was liable to bring out the loathing Boyle had for himself and all of humanity.

"…my mother never liked the cold, Charlie. She didn't take well to it, she said it killed something inside her when he regarded her that way. He told her he'd been testing her, tempting her like Satan, and that she had failed the test. He told her she had failed God… I'm not a religious man myself, but my mother – she fell for it, every word. I don't know, I've rarely been in the company of the man, and on the few occasions we have exchanged words I can't say that I took to him, or after him for that matter. I don't know, maybe he hypnotised her. Do you think that is possible, Charlie?"

"You'd be surprised at what's possible," Boyle replied.

"Maybe so..."

Elmer's voice fell away. Slowly, like the inching of the tide, Boyle realised that Elmer liked him. The thought gave him a small glow of satisfaction.

"He had her moved out of the parish before I was born, shunted from one council house to another. Pulling strings – he knows people – he treated her – us – like an inconvenience. Like so much baggage to be moved on… It wasn't easy, just me and the old dear, but I tell you what, Charlie – I still reckon I had it easier all those years than Stella."

Elmer paused then. This time the pause stretched and endured until it turned into a fat silence. Boyle could feel Elmer's presence behind him, willing him to say something, to fill the void he had opened.

Boyle was adept at stringing silence out, but maybe because he knew Elmer liked him, he decided to throw him a line.

"Who knows, Elmer, maybe it was easier for you. You know it seems to me that life isn't much more than a series of maybes and what ifs," Boyle said.

Elmer leaned forward in his seat so that his lips were close to Boyle's ear. Boyle looked at him sidewise. This close, and from this angle, Elmer was all nose and mouth.

"I need you to promise me something, Charlie," he said into Boyle's ear. "Will you do that?"

"Depends on what you're asking."

Elmer grunted then said, "I need you to take care of Stella."

"Take care of her? How can I take care of her? She doesn't want anything to do with me."

"Yeah, I know – it's a tricky one for sure, but even so I want you to take care of her, Charlie. Will you do that – will you take care of Stella?"

"Sure," Boyle said, "I'll take care of her." Thinking it didn't matter what he said. It was only words after all.

He felt the vibration of his phone in his pocket before he heard the new message alert. His body tensed. Whatever it was, the news would not be good.

It never was.

He wondered what would happen if he ignored it. Better still, what would happen if he opened the car door and tossed the phone away, leaving it to corrode in layers of autumnal debris. But even as he had the thought he knew he would never follow it through and so he took the phone out and opened the message.

Three words on the screen – *tick tock charlie* – and an attachment. He hesitated before opening it.

Was it still real if he didn't look?

Boyle looked and it was real.

The attachment contained, as he knew it would, photographs of Jenny. In the first, she was sitting on a bed, duvet pulled up to her armpits, smiling coyly for the camera. The fist tightened on his innards again, squeezing harder than before. He flicked to the next image. The duvet had been pulled aside, revealing her breasts. Jenny was laughing. As he flicked to the third, sweat popped on Boyle's brow and his gorge rose. His daughter was naked, legs spread, no smiles, no laughter.

Every muscle in Boyle's body clenched. For a moment he was nothing but a compressed ball, crowding in on himself, becoming tighter, harder. He fought to erase the images from his mind, but they were scorched on. A permanent reminder of everything that was wrong with him.

A hot flash of anger exploded through him. Elmer was talking, but Boyle couldn't hear him over the white noise buzzing in his ears. Hands shaking, he called Jenny's number, screaming into the phone when Friel answered.

Don't you touch her don'tyoufuckingtouchher if you do anything to her I will rip yourfuckinghead off doyouhearme I will rip your fucking head off-

144

On and on Boyle screamed threats delivered at fever pitch, words running into each other, spit flying from his mouth, his body flooded with adrenalin, mind spinning, anger churning his guts. He ranted until his juice ran dry and his mouth seized up and he couldn't think what else to say. And then the voice came from the other end.

Finished?

Boyle sucked in a lungful of stale car air. "Yes."

Have you got the goods?

Boyle raised his head and stared at the closed front door of the manse.

"I'm getting them now. Where will I take them to?" His voice weary.

You'll be told – don't worry about that. One more thing…

"What?"

Don't talk to me like that again – all you're going to do is make it worse for Jenny. Precious Jenny… I'm told she was good – very good - know what I mean, Charlie?

"Don't you-"

Uh-uh, Charlie. Best you keep a cool head. Now why don't you thank me for the advice.

Boyle chewed the inside of his face. When he spoke his voice strained through lips puckered tight as an arsehole.

"Thank you."

Chapter 32

Jenny dressed in the bedroom, pulling her clothes on quickly in case he returned and… *And what*, Jenny? She paused and looked at the door. What was she scared of? *Scared?* Yes, scared. She was scared. Scared of him coming back and of what he would do to her.

She could say no. Would that work? She hadn't wanted him to do what he'd done in the shower – but had she said no? She had thought the word, but had she said it aloud? She couldn't – physically she couldn't. Her mouth had been filled with water. She hadn't said it, hadn't been able to, but she had hit him, clawed at his back, tried to repel him. Her frantic protests had been taken by him as encouragement to thrust harder, deeper. Had he known what she meant? Had he understood and chosen to ignore?

Jenny, did he rape you? Is that what you are saying here?

The word brought her up short. It frightened her. She couldn't think straight, not with his presence - with the threat of him - so close by. She had to get out. First finish getting dressed, then she could walk out. She didn't have to say anything, she could just pick up her bag and go. That's it, keep it simple. No words, no arguments, no need to make excuses, just go.

She tied the laces on her Converse and stood up straight in front of the full-length mirror. Her face was tight. She looked upset. This was not good. Upset was weak, vulnerable. She had to look strong, calm, composed. She had to look like the kind of person Michael would not argue with.

She took a few deep breaths, and worked her jaw, stretching her face, driving out the scared rabbit look. She rolled her shoulders and stretched her arms, realising as she did so that she was effectively warming up the way she did before running. Running was her game plan, so why not? All limbered up, she walked to the door.

Heart pitter-patting, adrenalin flushing through her

system, she opened it and quickly orientated herself. The front door was along the hall to her left, the open plan living area to her right. If she forgot about her bag – abandoning her keys, phone, money, bank cards... – she could make a dash for the door.

"Hey," Michael said, "I was just going to come and get you. Pizza's ready."

He appeared at the kitchen island, pizza cutter in his hand, a smile on his face. They were in full view of each other. Jenny hesitated, thinking how weird it would be in the face of such hospitality to suddenly sprint down the hall and run out of the door.

"There's still some champagne left."

She stayed where she was, suddenly unable to move in any direction and when he brought a glass to her she automatically accepted it and allowed herself to be ushered through to the ultra-modern, oversized sofa.

Michael talked all the while about pizza toppings and watching a film, and about how it was good to occasionally just kick back and chill.

"Where's my bag?" she asked when he left a pause long enough.

"In the cupboard, there," he said, indicating with a nod. "Why? Do you need it?"

The small inflection of surprise in his voice put her further on the back-foot.

"I wanted to check my phone."

The words felt silly. Jenny felt confused.

"Aww, really? I was hoping we wouldn't do phones this weekend. Just imagine, Jenny - texting, no calls, no interference – just us here, together. Let's forget about the rest of the world for a while - what do you say?"

His reasonable tone knocked her out of kilter. A few moments ago she'd been considering making a sprint for the door – as in actually, physically running out of his flat with nary a backward glance. Now he was sitting beside her on the sofa, all spread out and relaxed like everything was normal, and she had a glass of champagne in her hand which made it look as though she was entirely at ease when all she could think was *get out, this is a mistake.*

"You used your phone." Her voice was smaller, weaker, than she wanted it to be. It sounded like she was apologising in advance for any offence she may cause.

"But that was between us, Jenny – the rest of the world didn't come into it. Never mind that – the pizza will be getting cold."

He sprang up, his lithe movements a reminder of his vigour and strength. Good, positive words, vigour and strength – except that on this occasion they were on the wrong side of the equation.

Now, she told herself, now was the time to stand up and say she was leaving. Better still, just get up and leave. But it seemed such a stark thing to do, so… rude in the face of a person serving you champagne and food. And now she wasn't exactly sure what had happened in the shower, was thinking that she must have misunderstood. Michael was acting like a loved-up boyfriend. His behaviour didn't stack with what was in her head. It didn't stack with the word *rape*. She didn't feel sure about anything now, not even her own judgement. Especially not her own judgement.

By the time her thoughts had gone around in circles and through hoops, she was still sitting where she'd started and Michael was back, with a plate and a napkin, saying that you couldn't beat a classic margherita and he hoped she liked stone bake and how he wasn't one for deep pan. Too much dough. He was talking a lot, smiling too, all happy. Made her think of a kid at a carnival, balloon in one hand, candy floss in the other, thinking life couldn't get any better and there she was in the Hall of Mirrors, not sure which way up anything went or how it all fitted together.

He held out the plate. She wondered if you could accept pizza from someone and then walk out on them. It seemed odd. She felt odd, but accepted the plate because it was right in front of her and she didn't know what else to do without causing a scene.

It contained two large triangles of cheese-drenched pizza. The smell curdled her stomach. He encouraged her to try a piece. She took a small bite.

"Good?"

She swallowed and nodded. She wanted to not be there, but didn't know how to make that happen.

Their actions were reflected in the blank television screen. It was a normal domestic scene of two people sitting on a sofa together eating pizza. There was nothing to indicate that one of them was trying to escape the other, or that minutes before that person thought she had been raped but now she wasn't sure. She felt tender *down there*, and felt all wrong inside, but now it seemed that they were simply two people eating pizza.

He did most of the talking. She replied, she engaged, realising as she nodded and attempted a smile or two that her instinct for survival was kicking in. Her thoughts and feelings had been confused by his breezy attitude. She had questioned herself, questioned her instincts, but underneath her confusion lurked the knowledge that more was going on here than she knew, and whatever it was, it wasn't good.

Chapter 33

"What do you think of Mickey Rourke?"

The confusion in Jenny's eyes interested him. He watched closely as she searched for the right answer. She reminded him of a scene in a nature documentary about an antelope being stalked by a leopard. The leopard was in the undergrowth. The antelope couldn't see the leopard, couldn't hear it and couldn't smell it, but despite all the couldn'ts, the antelope knew something bad was going down.

Jenny shrugged and wobbled her head a little. Just like the antelope, she knew something bad was going down, she just didn't know what. That time would come.

"I don't know much about him."

"Really? He was a huge star back in the day - you never seen *Barfly*?"

"No… I don't think so."

"C'mon Jenny, I thought you were a movie buff?"

"I never claimed to have watched every movie ever made."

"Yeah, but Mickey Rourke…"

Killian liked the way she now flinched when he touched her. She tried to cover it up but the suppressed quiver rippling through his fingertips gave her away.

"I've heard of him —"

"Yeah, he was one of the biggest movie stars of the 1980s – *Rumble Fish*, *Angel Heart*, and of course…" he trailed his fingers across her collar bone, dragging the neckline of her top so that her bra strap was exposed, "…the cinematic classic, *9 ½ Weeks*… have you seen *9 ½ Weeks*, Jenny?"

She shook her head.

"But you've heard of it, right?"

She squirmed and adjusted her top to cover her bra, taking the opportunity while she was at it to knock his hand away. Killian accepted the rejection, letting his hand fall thus far before working it into the space between the small of her back and the sofa. Once there he quietly tugged at the bottom of her top, pulling it up over the waistband of her jeans until his fingers were massaging her bare flesh.

Tiny gestures and small movements told the story of how uncomfortable the intimate gesture made Jenny feel, but after the things they had already done to each other – after the way she had willingly exposed herself to him – she was confused by her own unease. They were, after all, two adults engaging in a consensual sexual relationship, and so even though she didn't like it she just sat there taking it.

It was fascinating to observe and extremely tasty. By small increments, Killian shifted closer to her until her space had been usurped by their space. *See how she squirms…*

"It's about two people who are really into each other…" he said, his mouth close to the nape of her neck, nuzzling the damp hair under the roots of her pony tail. "They push the boundaries, Jenny… they take it to a different level. The things he does to her… the things she does to-"

Without warning, Jenny squirmed free and was suddenly on her feet in front of him. Killian carried on talking as his gaze wandered up the length of her body to her face.

"This film I'm talking about, Jenny, it's a classic… the things they did in it – think where we could take those ideas…"

She stared at him like he had started talking Mandarin. A tremble ran through her slender frame. He watched with interest to see what she would do next. He almost hoped she would bring the situation to a head by making a lunge for the door, but there was still amusement to be had.

"Let's go for a walk," she said. "I need some air."

She broke eye contact and went to the closet where he'd hung her jacket. Killian stood up, watching as she fetched it and put it on. Through this process, not once did she look at him. Not so much as a glance did she spare him, so totally engrossed in doing up her jacket was she. And then, finally, with herself all trussed up for the going of the outside, she spared him a glance.

"You coming?"

Killian grinned, but said nothing.

"Okay I'll go on my own." Her voice high and tight.

He wondered if she would make a play for her bag or forfeit it in her silly wee bid for freedom. No, she walked to the hall without stopping, still trying to pretend it was situation normal. He followed her to the door. He didn't hound her. There was no need. He watched as she turned the handle.

All those levers locked in tight and a keyhole with no key. What was she going to do? He let her fuss at it for a bit. She kept on turning the handle, all the while steadfastly refusing to look at him. Refusing to acknowledge that she was in situation abnormal.

Finally, bored with the charade, he put his hand on the door in front of her face and stared at her until she stopped worrying the handle and looked at him.

The situation was about to get a whole lot more interesting.

Chapter 34

Boyle sat very still for a moment, his lips tight and white, his fists curled. Pressure was building behind his eyes. From a thousand miles away came the sound of Elmer asking if he was okay. Boyle let the moment last until he couldn't take the pressure any more, until he couldn't stand to see the images seared on his mind for one second longer, and then he exploded out of the car.

He stormed to the front door of the manse, Elmer calling into the abyss behind him, *where are you going, Charlie? Charlie? Charlie? What are you doing?* On and on, looking for answers he was never going to get.

Boyle didn't stop to knock at the door. He burst into the house, a hurricane no-one had prepared for. The woman he'd glimpsed earlier appeared at a door, looking like a startled mouse.

"Where's Stella?" he demanded.

She pointed at the ceiling. Boyle took the stairs two at a time, pausing only when he got to the upper floor. A lamp sitting on an occasional table had been switched on, but the light it cast was miserable. Five closed doors, each hewn from dark wood, lined the hall.

"STELLA," Boyle roared.

The door furthest away opened. A tall man stepped into the hall, his eyes blazing even in the dim light.

"Who are you? What are you doing here?" He reared up at Boyle, his face the very definition of outrage, his voice suggesting he was a man used to having his questions answered.

Boyle reared right back, the two of them facing off like a pair of lean, mean grizzlies. "Where's Stella?"

"I'm here, Charlie."

Stella appeared in the doorway behind her father. At least he figured it was Stella, only this wasn't the version he was used to. This Stella looked like she'd had the life sucked out of her, nothing left behind but a husk so frail, so diminished, he could almost see right through her.

If he'd thought about it at all, Boyle would have said that he couldn't take any more pain, not now, not with those images of his daughter burning inside him, and yet the agony flared more intensely and, as always with him, anger followed. It boiled lava-hot inside him before erupting in a wave of incandescent fury. He grabbed a hold of the preacher and slammed him against the wall. He pulled his arm back ready to swing a punch, but Stella lunged at him, grabbing hold of his arm, her emptiness weighing him down.

"No, Charlie - not like this."

She yelled at him to stop, but every fibre, every sinew, in Boyle's body was screaming at him to drive his fist right into the preacher's face. That whatever was up with Stella, whatever it was that had zapped her juice, it was down to this man and he was going to pay for it. Boyle was going to make him pay.

All the screaming, inside and outside of him, seethed his brain. All he could feel was raw anger and searing pain. He was hurting, hurting bad, and he wanted to hurt someone else in turn. The preacher would do as well as any and better than most. He'd hurt Stella. It would be a pleasure to pound and pound and pound into him, punching until muscle and skin and flesh and bone were one bloody, pulpy mash.

All the while Boyle's fist was clenched and these thoughts were going through his head, Stella, was hanging on to him, begging him not to do it, saying that it wouldn't help Jenny.

Jenny.

The sound of her name said aloud brought those images back. Boyle wanted to punch the pain out of himself. But what about Jenny? What was happening to her right now while he was here in this miserable house with this miserable God botherer pressed up against the miserable wall.

The thought of what could be happening – probably was happening – to his daughter now at this very minute, drained the strength right out of him. The lava cooled as suddenly as it had erupted, forming into cold, hard rock inside him.

Jenny, he had to focus on Jenny.

Boyle launched the punch, directing it into the wall beside the preacher's head. The flare of pain, the breaking of skin, the birth of bruising, released the last of the heat.

Stella's hands were still on his punching arm as he lowered it. She was saying his name over and over and over, like she was trying to fight her way through to him.

Charlie Charlie Charlie Charlie Charlie Charlie Charlie Charlie Charlie…

Boyle slowly turned his head and looked at her. Her eyes were pleading with him, her lips moving. She still cared. When you stripped the rest away, she still cared.

"Let go of me."

An order issued. Boyle's gaze swivelled back to the minister. The stare that met him was cold, hard and intense. What kind of god would have this man as his envoy? Boyle let go of the fistful of shirt he was holding and stepped back. Following the order. His thoughts took a detour back to Elmer's tale of woe, wondering if maybe the man did have the power to hypnotise.

"Is everything alright?"

Boyle turned at the sound of a small voice. A voice not used to being heard. Drawn by the commotion and the need to know, the mouse had crept up the stairs behind him.

"Does it look alright?" Boyle asked.

The question startled her. There was a moment in which Boyle thought she would gather her skirts and run, but fair play to her, she gave him an answer though he had to strain his ears to hear it.

"No, not really."

"Oh for goodness sake," the words spat from the preacher's mouth, "go downstairs, Elizabeth, and phone the police. Tell them we have an intruder in our home – a man of violence."

This earned a snort from Boyle but the mouse nodded

and made to go.

"No mum – don't."

Where it had come from, Boyle did not know, but he was glad to hear some of the old steel back in Stella's voice. The mouse stopped, her confused gaze darting between husband and daughter. Stay or go?

"What she said," Boyle nodded his head at Stella.

The mouse blinked and stayed where she was.

"Who the hell are you?"

The preacher's voice was loud and sharp in Boyle's ear. Boyle really wanted to hit him. Instead, he looked at Stella.

"Have you got what we came here for?"

"How dare you ignore-"

"Have you got them?" Boyle repeated.

"No." Stella's face was tight.

"What? Why not - where are they?"

Rage rising, tendons popping, and that unbearable pressure at the back of his eyes, making him want to lash out, to dispense pain.

"He's got them."

"What?" Boyle grabbed the preacher by the throat and slammed him against the wall again.

"No Charlie – ease off. Please – we need him to tell us where they are."

Boyle squeezed tighter. *One, two,* the preacher's eyes bulged... *three, four,* eleven pounds of pressure... *five, six,* on each carotid artery for ten... *seven, eight,* seconds and the preacher would be out cold.

Stella yelled, the mouse squealed. The preacher gasped as Boyle released his grip.

"Elizabeth – go - phone - the – " The words wheezed out of him.

"No mum – don't."

Stella pushed her face up close to her father's. They were, Boyle thought, a warped mirror-image of each other.

"We need that bag, father, and its contents – a young woman's life depends on it."

The preacher pursed his lips and regarded his daughter with hard eyes, when he spoke his voice was hoarse.

"You always were a liar, Stella. A deceitful girl with a foul mind."

"No father, I was just a child… foul things were done to me – but you know that, don't you?"

"I don't know what you're talking about."

"I think you do."

Boyle looked from one to the other. The preacher directed the same intense look at Stella he had given Boyle, but Stella mirrored it right back at him. The preacher blinked first. Something was going down between them. What it was Boyle did not know, but whatever it was, it was doing Stella a power of good. All the energy was going her way. She was not see-through anymore. Now it was the minister who looked like he was being hollowed out.

Behind him, the mouse murmured in the shadows, her small voice asking what was going on. The words barely whispered, as though she did not want anyone to hear for fear they would answer.

"You really don't want the police involved, father."

"You wouldn't dare." The words were half-asked, riding on a voice almost as small as his wife's.

"Don't test me on it." Stella's voice was gunmetal grey. "You might know my secrets, father, but I know plenty of yours."

"Is that me you're talking about?" Elmer appeared behind the mouse, about four times as large, and plenty louder.

"What's he doing here?" the minister hissed.

"You're just a minor indiscretion, Elmer. Our father has much darker secrets than you." Stella glanced at Boyle, "Take a look in there."

She indicated the room she'd come out of.

Boyle went in, Elmer at his back, and took the look he'd been told to take.

A room simply furnished can also be comfortable. This was not such a room. It was large yet contained only the barest essentials, and those, with spindly legs, scuffs and worn-through varnish, had an ill air about them. The impression was of scant little, grudgingly provided.

A threadbare rug by the bed had been pulled back, a rectangle of dark, varnished floorboard removed.

"Stella's hidey-hole," Elmer said.

Boyle got down on his hands and knees and felt inside the void.

"It's not hiding anything now."

They went back to the hall. Stella had evidently returned to full strength. The preacher's face was pinched. His complexion such that if he'd been a corpse, Boyle would have been worried for his health.

Of the mouse, there was no sign.

"I'm sorry, Charlie. I thought they'd be safe there. It was my secret place," she glanced at her father. "At least, I thought it was my secret place... but today I found out that he knew about it – that he'd known about it all along."

Boyle's fingers curled as he eyeballed the preacher. "Where's the bag?"

The preacher stared back. His face had shut down. Boyle could have tried beating the answer out of him, but this was a man used to keeping secrets and he wasn't for giving up this one. The temptation was to beat him anyway, but as that would not do Boyle's standing with Stella any good, he kept his furled fists tight into his side.

"Is this what you're looking for?"

Boyle turned to see the mouse holding a black holdall. He glanced at Stella. She nodded. Boyle relieved the mouse of the bag and checked inside. It was full of black velvet pouches. Elmer whistled as Boyle checked the contents of half a dozen of them – diamonds sparkled in rings, necklaces, bracelets.

"Are they really real?"

Elmer's eyes were so wide, Boyle almost laughed. "They're real alright. And I hope they are all here. You weren't tempted, were you?" he looked at the preacher.

"Did you take anything?" Stella asked.

"I'm not a thief." The words forced through tight lips.

"Maybe not, but you are a lot of other things."

Boyle zipped up the bag and handed it to Elmer. He strode across the hall and stood nose-to-nose with the preacher. He waited, letting the other man get properly uncomfortable with his proximity, and the implied threat, before speaking in a low growl.

"Just so you know, if you did take anything, it will come back on you big, bad and very, very unpleasant. You got that?"

The preacher twitched a nod. Boyle stood down.

"I'm out of here." He looked at Stella and Elmer. They looked at each other.

"We're coming with you," Elmer said.

"We?" Boyle looked at Stella. She nodded.

"I've got nothing better to do."

"What about you?" Boyle asked the mouse.

The mouse looked at her husband. The preacher was all uptight and emptied out at the same time.

"I'll be fine," she said.

The three of them headed to the stairs.

"You will burn in hell for your filthy lies, Stella."

The preacher's last stand was a pathetic affair, the fire and brimstone gone from his voice.

"I thought hell wasn't a real place, dad." Elmer said.

Boyle looked at him. *Dad?* Elmer winked.

"It exists alright, and that's where you are heading – all of you."

Boyle stopped at the half-landing and looked up at the empty shell of a man.

"See you there, preacher."

Chapter 35

Jenny tried to swallow her panic as she turned the handle again. The door was definitely locked - there was no sign of a key and Michael was right beside her. What now - what to say – how to get away – how?

Michael put his hand on the door in front of her face. Though it was pointless to do so, she continued to turn the handle. This tiny action was all that separated her between now and whatever was to come next. She didn't want to go there. She wanted to reverse time, not go forward. Go back, back, back.

The pale landscape of his hand lay before her - faint freckles, blue veins, clean, clipped nails. As he flexed his fingers she noted the suggestion of ligaments, tendons, and muscles at work.

She tried not to flinch when he took his hand from the door and placed it on her shoulder. And when he guided her by the slightest of squeezes, the lightest of prods, turning her away from the door until her body was facing his, she put up no resistance.

He stretched his thin lips into a smile. She forced her facial muscles into position, smiling in return. She mustn't give anything away. She had to be strong. She mustn't panic. She had to focus.

"It's cold outside, Jenny. Let's stay in. Just you and me together. We can cosy up on the sofa, watch a movie, finish the pizza. There's plenty left."

"Sounds good." Her voice seemed to come from far away, to belong to someone else.

Michael turned her around and steered her back to the living room. There was no doubt now – she was trapped here. She knew it, he knew it, and he knew that she knew it, but there was yet a game to play. A pretence to be kept up. Perhaps, if she played the game well enough, there would be a way out, but what she must not do was excite him. She had to play it cool, keep his blood down.

"Take your jacket off."

She did as she was told and handed it to him. He hung it back in the closet beside his own and as he did so she saw what she had seen before, but only now did she pay attention and wonder.

There were only the two jackets. Hers and Michael's. There was nothing else in there – no hats, no scarves, no boots or shoes or any other jacket, or indeed any of the myriad of things a person might keep in a cupboard.

She cast a fresh gaze around the room. Not minimalist. Empty.

His phone rang. He took it out of his pocket and looked at the screen.

"You said no phones."

He put his finger to his lips to hush her then answered the call. Fine, a new rule then. Surely if it was okay for him then it was okay for her. She went to the wall of cupboards and began opening doors, looking for her bag. He carried on with his conversation, made no attempt to stop her.

Sweat prickled in Jenny's armpits. A knot formed in her stomach. Every drawer, every cupboard, every shelf was empty, empty, empty. The knot tightened a little more as each bare space was revealed.

There was no evidence of this being anyone's home. Michael did not live here. Nobody lived here. It was a show home. An empty space to which he had brought her, not for romance, not to cement their relationship, but to use her, hurt her, harm her in some way. *But why? Why her? To what end?* None of it made any sense.

Finally, she found her bag. She took it from the cupboard in which it had been stowed and opened it, looking for her phone. It wasn't in its usual place and so she looked again, and again, rummaging more frantically each time. No phone. She had brought it with her, she knew she had brought it. There was no way she had lost it.

She looked at Michael. He was still on his call, giving short yes-no answers, but he was watching her, a smile curling his lips, enjoying her discomfort.

The game play was up. It was time to face him off. She sucked in deep breaths, trying to calm herself, trying to steady her nerves. The adrenalin in her system had wasted her legs, she felt unsteady, but she could not let fear get the better of her.

"Okay… yes… I'll take care of it."

He came towards her as the call came to an end, his gaze locked on hers, a familiar amused look in his eyes. Was it really so recently she had found it attractive? Now it repelled her. Made her feel sick to her core.

She pulled her shoulders back and raised her chin. *Show no fear, show no fear, show no* – Michael lashed out, still smiling as his hand connected with the side of her face.

The impact knocked her from her feet, sending her into a spin. She had no control, she was ungrounded, lost. She landed hard. Michael stood over her as she lay dazed on the floor. He was still smiling, still on the phone, bringing the call to an end.

She touched her face where his blow had landed. Her cheek was numb. When she looked at her hand there was blood on her fingers.

"Looks like you've got a split lip."

She looked up to see him taking photographs of her.

She worked her jaw, opening her mouth, but there was a disconnection between her brain and her tongue as she struggled to comprehend her situation. Finally, as he was fiddling with his phone, she managed to get the words out.

"What are you doing?"

"My job."

He answered without looking at her, his eyes on the screen.

Keeping a wary eye on him, she got to her feet. She did not know this man, not in the sense that one person can never really know another, rather in the sense that she simply did not know him. He was a stranger. A stranger who meant her harm.

She inched towards the door.

"Where are you going?" He looked up from his phone.

"I'm leaving."

"I don't think so."

"Yes, I am." She struggled to keep her tone even, her voice sure. "Whatever game you are playing – it's over."

He shook his head and smiled his creepy smile. "No, Jenny. We're just getting started."

Chapter 36

Lenny Friel sat back in his big leather chair and took a minute to enjoy the moment. He had his mojo back and then some. He'd long suspected that Michael Killian was a psychopath and it was a pleasure to be proved correct. Domesticated psychopaths were always handy to have around.

Now that it was a problem taken care of, or at least as good as taken care of, Friel could admit it - this whole Boyle situation had given him a wobble. He had been worried. And he'd been right to be worried. You had to fight a lot harder to stay at the top than you did to get there in the first place, but Friel always had been a fighter. That's how he'd earned the loyalty of his people. Sure, wasn't his steadfast lieutenant, Bobby Big Cheeks, out there now doing his bidding. The ones trying to break into Friel's territory – the big men wannabes - were getting their arses kicked at this very moment. Oh happy days.

He looked again at the latest pictures Michael had sent him. The girl staring at the camera, eyes wide and scared, lip split, blood dribbling down her chin. He snorted, wondering what would happen if he gave Michael free rein. Just how far would he go…

Time to pick off the scab and give the wound a poke.

Boyle answered on the first ring.

I told you not to hurt her – I've got them – I've got the diamonds.

Friel smiled, enjoying the barely controlled rage in Boyle's voice. The man was on the edge. It would be a delight to push him over.

"She's fine, Charlie. It's just a split lip. No need to get all het up."

The outraged father boiled at the other end.

"Settle down, Charlie… I can send the other kind of pictures if you prefer?"

Boyle went from frothing to begging, there might even have been a little weeping in the mix. Friel wrinkled his nose.

"Come on now, Charlie. Don't humiliate yourself. No harm done. She's fine, and she'll stay fine… just as long as you hand over what you owe."

Bored with Boyle's snivelling, Friel gave him directions to the yard and hung up.

He wondered how much of Boyle's soul had been eaten up in the process of pleading. The man was a car crash. An existence that wretched surely wasn't worth living. It would be nothing less than a mercy to put him out of his misery.

Friel let out a satisfied sigh. It was all coming together. Boyle had the goods, and Friel had the goods on Boyle. Sammy's debt would be paid and then some. Boyle would get his, the daughter would get hers and everyone would be shit-scared of Lenny Friel just the way they ought to be.

From outside came the clang of the metal gate. Friel checked the time. Spanish Tony shutting up shop behind the workers on the legit payroll. A few minutes later came the sound of approaching footsteps. The door to the office opened and Spanish Tony walked in.

"You wanted to see me, boss?"

"Boyle's on his way – make sure he gets a warm welcome."

Chapter 37

"You okay?"

Boyle was about as un-okay as it was possible to get. The exchange with the preacher had served as a mental block. His anger and loathing for the man had given him something else to think about, to react to, but now he was back in the car. Not even driving. Just sitting, with nothing in his head but those images of Jenny.

His hands had balled into punches bursting to land. His face had fisted, nose, teeth, eyes, all scrunched up tight. Lips white. Teeth straining against them. An intense pressure had built up inside him, threatening to split his skin. Threatening to tear him apart.

If it had been Elmer doing the asking, Boyle might have grabbed him by the throat, but Elmer was sitting right back in the rear seat, keeping out of it. He was nowhere near as daft as he looked. It was Stella talking to him. Stella, who wanted nothing more to do with him, was glancing at him and asking if he was okay.

He wanted to answer. He wanted to tell her what was going on, about what they were doing to Jenny. He needed the release, but the words wrapped themselves around his throat, threatening to strangle him.

"Charlie, talk to me."

"They're... they're doing things to her."

The words dryly expelled from his mouth in broken pieces.

"Charlie, listen to me – are you listening?"

Boyle twitched a nod. He was staring straight ahead. Movement was a risk. If he let anything go, chances were the whole lot would be unleashed. That time would come, but not yet.

"We'll get her – do you understand – together, we'll get her. She'll be okay, she's tough."

Jenny – tough? Was she?

A movie reel played in his head. Images of them running

on the beach at Nairn. Father and daughter, splashing each other, laughing together. The two of them going somewhere in the car. Destination long forgot, the getting there becoming the memory. Listening to Bowie's *Hunky Dory*. Singing along at the top of their voices to *Life On Mars?*

Was that girl tough? Maybe, maybe she was. She had to be. They'd find out soon enough.

"There's something inside her, Charlie. She'll find it and that will get her through."

Boyle took a deep breath and let some of the tension loose.

"I'm going to kill them – the people who took her. I'm going to kill them."

Chapter 38

"Who are you?"

"You know who I am, Jenny."

Everything had flipped, the change immediate, the effect profound. The thin-lipped smile she had found so attractive before was now repulsive to her. His strength, his physical fitness, which she had so recently admired, was now a threat. The man she had found so sexually attractive, now filled her with fear.

He slowly circled around her, blocking her access to the door. Not that she could get out anyway, not without a key. He knew that. So this was a psychological move. Intended to intimidate her, to show her he was in control. The thing was, even though she knew what he was doing, it worked. She felt trapped. But cornered animals tended to fight back.

"I don't know you. I don't know who you are."

Her voice was steadier now. She adapted quickly. She did not understand why she was here, but she had to deal with the fact that she was. She must remain calm, keep thinking, talk to him, try to establish a connection. Whatever he was up to, whatever it was he wanted, it would be better for her if he saw her as a person, if they had a bond. It was straight out of Hostage Survival 101.

"Sure you do, Jenny. You know me. I'm Michael. We met at The Classic."

He stepped towards her. She stepped back, towards the kitchen island. She must be vigilant, seek opportunities and exploit them. And if the worst came to the worst she would gouge and scratch and pull hair. She would fill her fingernails with his cells, splatter herself in his DNA, so that if it came to it – if he killed her - her body would have a story to tell.

Murder, was she really thinking murder? She watched him, prowling, circling, closing in. He was a predator preparing to pounce. Yes, she thought, the word she had in mind was murder, but knowing she could get to him even if he killed her gave her strength. Whatever she did, however this played out, she would not make it easy for him.

"You like films, I like films... *Roman Holiday, Texas Chainsaw Massacre, Straw Dogs...* you know - feel-good movies."

She thought back to meeting him at the cinema. It had seemed so... perfect. Too perfect. The pieces clicked into place.

"That's why you went to The Classic, wasn't it – to find someone?"

He laughed. "Not quite, Jenny. Not just someone..."

The good news? He had engaged. Her efforts amused him, he was playing along. Maybe he wanted to show how clever he was. He stared at her as she spoke. His intense blue eyes looking into her. Into *her...*

"It was me, wasn't it? You went there for me."

"That's right, Jenny – I went there for you."

He'd moved closer. She had to tilt her head now to look him in the eye. She inched away, backing herself into the kitchen island.

"But I don't understand – why me?"

She felt her way along the marble counter. Maybe she could work her way around it, somehow get it between them. A barrier – Michael on one side, she on the other. And then what?

Don't overthink it. Just do it.

"Does there have to be a why?"

She had to keep moving, had to keep going. Had to keep him engaged. As long as he was engaged, she would be okay.

"But there is a why, Michael. There's a reason you picked me. I know there is."

Her hand encountered an object on the counter – the pizza cutter.

"Can't two people just fall in love, Jenny? Does it have to be any more complicated than that?"

Smart-assing her. Thinking he was funny. Good. If he was laughing at her, his guard was down. All she needed was a break, just a tiny break.

Her fingers closed on the pizza cutter handle as he closed the gap between them. He filled the space with his presence, muscle, sinew and strength looming over her. He looked down at her. Mocking her, enjoying his moment.

"Jenny, I'm just a boy standing in front of a-"

She swung her arm, aiming at his face. He juked out of the way, but not fast enough. The blade of the pizza cutter connected with his cheekbone. Jenny drove it on with as much force as she could muster. She felt the change in resistance as the blade wheeled from the skin stretched taught over his cheekbone to the yielding jelly of his eye.

Michael instinctively covering his wounded eye and howled. She had a moment, but only a moment.

Jenny ran.

He was after her in a beat. If she went to the front door he'd be on her. There was nothing to be done there, not now, not yet, not without a key. She had to buy time. Try to figure something out. She fled to the bedroom and slammed the door.

No lock on this door. She grabbed a chair and wedged it under the handle just as Michael crashed into the other side. She jumped, but the chair held. Michael rattled on the handle. Jenny ran to the window and pulled the curtains aside. She expected to be looking down on the street, but the window looked onto the stark wall of the neighbouring building. No windows to view, no good Samaritans on hand. The street was a hard left, with her face pressed against the glass. No matter, she could still call for help. Maybe climb out. Scream, yell. Do something.

The window would not open. She looked for a key. None to be seen. Maybe it had fallen on the floor, but of course it hadn't. The window had been locked, the key removed. She may have little idea of who Michael was or what he wanted, but this she did know – he planned, and he planned with care. The thought was not a reassuring one.

The chair creaked as he battered into the door. It was holding, but it wouldn't last. She looked around the room. She could use the bed to block the door, that is if the bed was even moveable, but she would still be trapped in the room. A quick glance in the en-suite confirmed what she already knew. It was internal. No windows, no way out. Not unless she flushed herself down the toilet.

Michael pounded and rattled at the door. The chair splintered and groaned.

Chapter 39

"Why are you doing this?"

"Doing what?"

"Helping me."

"Maybe it's Jenny I'm helping."

"You don't know her."

"She's a young woman in trouble. That's all I need to know."

"That's noble of you."

Stella slid Boyle a look. He told her sorry, the sound low, the word small as he felt. Though it was still there, the anger inside him had subsided. It was now a compressed weight sitting in the pit of his stomach. It couldn't be maintained at peak level, not without the wiring inside him burning up.

The ebbing of his rage had left him diminished. He felt pathetic and useless. A waste of skin.

"I never really knew you, did I?" He said the words to prove that he still existed, and maybe to provoke a reaction.

Stella kept her eyes on the road and said nothing.

Elmer leaned forward. "Nobody really knows Stella, not even me. Do they, sis?"

This earned a twitch of Stella's lips a generous person might have described as a smile.

"You least of all, Elmer." Her tone was flat, giving nothing away but Elmer hooted anyway, as easy with his laughter as he was with his fists. He spoke again when his mirth had simmered down.

"Maybe so, Stell, but I know you, Charlie."

"Sure you do." Boyle going along with the ride because the alternative path for his thoughts was a bitter one.

"Oh yeah. Man, you're an easy read – at least to me you are. A wide open book."

"So what is it you think you know, Elmer?"

"That you're a hound dog, Charlie, nothing but a big old hound dog. Always on the prowl, sniffing around for something tasty. I bet that nose of yours has got you into a lot of trouble. In fact, I bet you've been in trouble with women all your life."

Boyle didn't know whether to be pissed off or amused at the accuracy of Elmer's description. The lunk was nowhere near as daft as he looked. As Boyle's cup was already overflowing with ire, he settled for amused. What else you gonna do, sit there and cry?

Boyle didn't have a tear in him.

"Not all my life," he said.

"Settled down for a while, huh?"

"Yup."

"Jenny's mum?"

"Yup."

"Couldn't keep it zippered though, could you Charlie?"

"Nope."

"Marriage break down?"

"Yup."

"Sorry to hear that, Charlie. Divorce is a messy and hurtful situation for all concerned."

"It certainly is, Elmer."

"You have anything to do with this particular messy situation, Stella?"

Boyle couldn't help but grin as Stella narrowed her eyes.

"You've got that one all wrong, Elmer," Boyle said. "My marriage was over long before I met Stella."

"Glad to hear it. Not about your marriage, Charlie. Sorry about that, even if it was your own doing. Just glad to hear that Stella isn't a marriage-wrecker."

"It was marriage that wrecked me, Elmer, not the other way around." Stella spoke through tight lips.

"Sorry, sis. Didn't mean to stir it all up. I never did like Frank. Ha, I suppose you could call that the understatement of the year."

Seemed Frank Valentine had no fans in the car and as no-one was going to do it for him, Elmer berated himself.

"I know, I know – I shouldn't speak ill of the dead and all that, but sis, why did you ever marry him?"

Mentally, Boyle sat up. He'd long wanted to know the answer to this question. There were few people in the world Boyle actively liked so his dislike for Frank was hardly surprising, but what had Stella ever seen in him?

He sat quietly. If he pretended he wasn't there, she just might answer Elmer's question.

He sat quiet, Elmer sat quiet, and Stella sat quiet. At least she did for a while, and then finally…

"He had charm, Elmer, and I couldn't see past it. At least not at first. Besides, he was my escape from home, my way out."

Though there was a chance she'd clam up on him, Boyle risked a question.

"You were still living at home when you married Frank?"

Stella nodded.

"She was a child-bride, Charlie. Still in her teens when Prince Charming came along."

"He was charming – he wooed me, and I fell for it. I didn't know any better."

"Just like our mothers fell for dear old dad's charm."

"Yeah, well dear old dad was short on charm today." Boyle said.

"He can turn it on like a tap," Stella said, "when he wants – or needs – to."

"I guarantee our mothers weren't the only ones to fall for it. Stella and me? We've most likely got brothers and sisters all across Perthshire and beyond. What do you say, sis?"

"Wouldn't surprise me."

"Might even have some right here in old Stirling town. All those lights, all those people. I wonder how far dad spread his seed."

"Elmer?"

"Yeah, Stella?"

"Shut up. You're making me feel sick."

"Sorry, sis."

Boyle looked out the passenger window at the blanket of lights spread out beneath a floodlit Stirling Castle. Between the twinkling lights of the town and the illuminated fortress lay the hulking, dark mass of the extinct volcano on which the castle had been built.

Boyle curled his fists and returned his gaze to the road ahead. One way or another, it would all be over in an hour.

Chapter 40

There came a loud crack as the chair splintered. Any minute now Michael would be through the door like the Big Bad Wolf. There was no more pretending, the game was up. Whatever harm he meant to do her would be done unless she hurt him first.

Jenny scrambled around the room looking for a weapon. The chair wedged against the door had a twin. She lifted it. It was light enough. She raised it higher, tried swinging it, thinking she could use it to whack him when he broke through, but it was unwieldy, the balance all wrong. He'd have her off her feet long before it connected with his skull.

She thought about locking herself in the shower room. That would buy her some time for sure, but she would be cornered in a smaller place. No, there had to be another way, had to be something else. Had to be.

She could have hit him over the head with a lamp, but there were no lamps, only the stupid, subtle, built-in lighting. There were no stray objects of any description in the room. She opened wardrobe doors, pulled out drawers. Empty, empty, all empty. She'd called it right – he didn't live here at all. The knowledge brought no relief, but it hardened the pearl of determination in her gut. Whatever it was he had planned for her, she wasn't going down without a fight.

Michael thudded against the door. Panic flared, her heart-rate increased. She looked but she could not see. Pillows. Lots of pillows. She could suffocate him if only he was lying down. Getting him down was the problem. Everywhere she looked she drew a blank. This room, this flat, was no more than a well-appointed prison cell. Michael had planned this and planned it well.

She spun around seeing the same things over and over. Stupid to keep doing the same thing yet expect a different result. At this rate she would be spinning like a top when he burst through but she mustn't give up. Mustn't make it easy for him.

Ignoring the creaking and splintering of the chair, blanking out the sound of Michael grunting as he thudded into the door, Jenny stopped turning and closed her eyes for a count of five. She opened them and looked at the room afresh. There had to be something.

The wardrobe doors hung open, revealing the emptiness inside. Her gaze slid past them, stopped, returned. Heart rate leaping again, this time with excitement, Jenny ran to the nearest cupboard. Nothing there but fixtures and fittings. One of the fittings being a chrome hanging rail. She grasped hold of the rail and gave it a shake. It held fast. End sockets cradled the rail. She pushed upwards but there was no give. She tried again. Nothing. Behind her, the holding chair cracked and moaned. Sweat flowed, blood coursed, her breathing increased. Short, shallow breathes. She paused, forcing herself to breathe deeper, calming herself. Hyperventilating would do her no good.

She tried the next wardrobe, grabbing hold of the rail. There was movement. She tried again. The rail was loose at one end. On the other side of the door, Michael cursed as his phone rang out. Jenny stepped inside the wardrobe and forced the rail up out of its cradle at the loose end. The phone stopped ringing and started again. Michael swore and battered the door. The other side of the rail held fast. Jenny twisted it back and forth, working it loose.

"Let me in, Jenny. You're only making it worse for yourself."

He yelled over the incessant sound of his phone. She glanced at the chair, willing it to hold for a few seconds more. She worked at the rail, pulling and pushing. She staggered, almost stumbled, as it came free in her hand.

She held it in the manner of a baseball bat and gave it a couple of test swings.

"Yesss." She grinned without smiling, hissing the word under her breath. Now she had something she could use.

"How Michael – how am I making it worse for myself?"

He answered with a thud. She ran to the door, positioning

herself with her back to the wall beside it. She swung the pole in time with his thuds, getting into his rhythm. Preparing to use it against him.

Ready, steady, at the ebb of his thuds she unhooked the chair from the handle and pushed it aside. Resistance reduced, Michael came hurtling into the bedroom with the force of his next assault. Jenny swung the pole and caught him a crack across the back. He squawked and lurched before catching his balance and whirling on her.

She gasped at the sight of his wounded eye. The lids were closed, swollen together, the cut from the pizza slicer a maniacal tear running across his cheekbone from the eye socket. The sensation of yielding jelly beneath turning metal came back to her in an instant, sucking the fight out of her. Fluid released from his injured eye had dried to a crystallised trail on his cheek. The metal rod quivered in her grasp. She'd been ready to beat him as he came through the door, but face-to-face was a different game. A game she had no stomach for.

Michael looked at her with his good eye. His gaze was as clear and blue as ever, only now instead of a kindred spirit, she saw nothing in its depths but a cold abyss. He glanced at the pole then back at her and shook his head to the beat his words.

"Oh, Jenny, Jenny, Jenny – what have we got here?"

She tightened her grasp so that the bones of her fingers were rolling against each other. She tensed, ready to strike, telling herself she could do it. She. Could. Do. It.

Michael sneered and took a step towards her. Jenny raised the pole. Across the head, she had to whack him across the head. She had to do it repeatedly. Get him down and keep him down. Crack his skull if that's what it took – and it would. Beat him down, then retrieve the keys and get out of there.

His sneer twisted and writhed like a snake on hot coals. It coiled out from his face and wrapped itself around her throat. She tried to catch a breath as it constricted her windpipe, crushing cartilage, shredding the mucosa lining. This he could do with a look.

In that moment, Jenny knew fear. She was entirely trapped in the moment. At no other time in her life had she been so acutely aware of the here and now. Held tight by his crazed stare, a tsunami of fear loomed over like a wall of water threatening to engulf her.

The familiar ring tone of Michael's phone scythed through the air. Holding her with his gaze, he took it from his pocket and answered it.

"Yeah – yeah – yeah – I know." His good eye on her as he spoke. His one-eyed gaze never wavering.

Between the gaps in his words she could hear the angry buzz of a distant voice. She could not make out what it was saying, but the tone rang out true and clear. It was persistent, insistent, full of rage. A furious wound cutting through the ether.

"Relax…. Yeah, I know – I know…. we're on our way."

Michael's neutral tone salving the lesion, closing the gash.

Jenny did not understand the finer details of her predicament, but this much she understood: Michael's calm tone and the resulting appeasement of the other voice were bad news for her.

She swung the pole, aiming for his head.

Chapter 41

Friel paced the Portakabin. When Michael finally answered, Friel ranted and raved down the phone at him. Boyle was on his way with the diamonds – *where was the girl?*

Michael's tone was calm, verging on relaxed. It infuriated Friel even more. Michael either did not grasp or was wilfully ignoring the urgency of the situation. If Friel didn't know better, he would have thought that Killian was on the wind-up. Maybe he was on the wind-up. A vein throbbed in Friel's temple. He'd think about this later when he had head space.

Once was, he could have cut Michael – or any of the rest of them - down to size without pausing to draw breath. But not now. The Boyle situation had filled him to capacity. Maybe it wasn't just that - maybe he was losing his edge. Man in his situation with no edge was no man at all.

"GET HER HERE NOW!"

He roared the words, his red fury turning incandescent white when Michael told him to relax.

"Relax?"

Friel shrieked the word before catching on to himself. Just as well Bobby Big Cheeks wasn't here to witness his meltdown. They traded gossip these guys, yakking it up like a bunch of old women in the steamie. He didn't need this kind of talk going around. Didn't need anyone saying that Lenny Friel was losing his grip, that he wasn't the man he used to be. That his mojo was gone, leaving him as limp and useless as a used condom. It was all screwed up. He was all screwed up.

Lenny Friel never lost his cool, never tipped his hand.

Except that now he did and he hadn't just tipped his hand, this was a game of 52 card pick-up. He was out of control, everything running away from him and he didn't like it. He liked it even less that people he relied on – people he had thought loyal – were wavering and havering and letting him down. The walls of his empire were already crumbling and now the very foundations were shaking.

This fear, this loss of control, it wasn't like him and that scared him even more. He sucked a few sharp breaths through his nose.

C'mon, Lenny, he told himself. Get a grip.

We're on our way.

He hung up. Michael had finally told him what he wanted to hear, but Friel did not care for the tone in which it had been delivered. He especially didn't like the fact that it had taken several failed calls before Michael picked up in the first place. Something wasn't right. The *wasn't rightness* bothered him, but there was no time to think about it now. Later, he would deal with all things Michael Killian later - for now all he needed to know was that the girl was being brought to him. Soon, very soon, Boyle would get what was coming to him. He would be humiliated and then destroyed.

Only then, once Friel had the diamonds and Boyle had met his unhappy ever after, would Friel start taking care of the business closer to home. He'd occasionally allowed himself to think of Michael as a surrogate son, but that didn't give the boy the right to treat him with the same disdain Friel's daughter dished out.

Friel was at a loss with her. Debs should be taking care of her, sorting her out. She needed her face straightening. But Debs was never around. Always out with her sister or the salon girls, or... he didn't even know anymore.

Maybe she was at it. Shagging around behind his back.

He stood motionless at the thought. Debs, betray him like that? He couldn't see it... besides, the bloke would have to be stupid. Friel had eyes and ears everywhere. If it was going on, he'd know about it and Casanova would end up with two broken legs and a swim in the Clyde for his trouble.

But would he know about it? He only knew what he knew. He didn't know what he didn't know. He didn't know what they were keeping from him.

Were they keeping things from him?

He shook his head, trying to loosen the thoughts and

throw them away. If he let paranoia get to him he was done. He might as well put a bullet to his head here and now. Debs was faithful, she always had been. Bobby Big Cheeks was utterly reliable. Told him everything he heard on the street. Sure, he was out there now fixing things. Spanish Tony was the best kind of loyal – the too stupid to think for himself kind. And Michael was…

He still wasn't sure about Michael.

Stop lying to yourself. You know what Michael is all about. Michael is you, Lenny. He is you… a younger, fitter, hungrier version of you. But what is it he's hungry for?

Friel looked around his office. When all was said and done, it was nothing more than a hut in a breaker's yard. Was this it then? Was this everything he had dreamed of, desired, worked for?

Of course not. There was the flat – sorry, make that luxury duplex apartment with city and river views. There was that.

There had been mucho excitement when they first moved in. Debs had been so excited, she'd been all over him, lavishing her love on him, praising him, adoring him. She'd squealed and purred over soft furnishings. She had devoted herself to the art of spending big money in fancy stores, but she'd got used to the good life pretty damn quick.

Debs had loved it then but it seemed she was never at home now. And though his daughter often was at home even when she wasn't meant to be, for all the interaction she had with him he might as well have been alone. He hung about the place like a bad smell, looking down the river at where he'd come from, thinking it wasn't all that far to fall and sooner or later he was going to take the tumble.

But not yet. Not yet.

Chapter 42

Jenny telegraphed her intention so far in advance Michael had time to wonder where she'd found the pole. As it swung towards his head he recognised it as a clothes rail. Ten out of ten for ingenuity, Jenny. Nil points for execution. For one thing, she was too close to him. For another, the angle she came at him was all wrong. She wouldn't have done damage even if she had connected with his head. But these were minor details in comparison to her lack of conviction in the action. Halfway through her swing she lost herself the battle.

He could see it in her eyes. She didn't have it in her to carry it through. She didn't have the killer instinct, not even when it came to defending herself. She'd caught him good with the pizza slicer, but that one action was all she had. When she saw the damage she'd done to him, she caved in. There was no more fight in her. Sweet Jenny Boyle was all flight. The pity for her was she had no place to fly.

He grinned, enjoying the horror on her face as she gazed at the mess she'd made of his. It hurt like a bastard, *throb, throb, throb*, but adrenalin was a wonderful thing. The rush from it could get you through a lot.

Michael dodged the cumbersome arc of Jenny's aim and grabbed both of her wrists in one fist, squeezing veins and fine bones together until the tips of her fingers bulged and she loosened her grasp on the pole.

As it hit the carpet he pulled her close. She tried to avert her gaze, but he gripped her face and turned it towards his own.

"Take a good look, Jenny. See what you've done?"

He watched, fascinated, as the pupils in her eyes dilated then contracted.

"Aww sweetheart, you're shaking. Don't be scared. I'll take care of you."

He leant into her and nuzzled her neck. Her breathing was heavy and shallow. Sweat sheened her skin. He could smell the fragrance of the toiletries she'd used, shampoo, shower gel. Beneath the scent of products ran the fine perfume of fear. He licked her neck. He wanted to know what fear tasted like. She shuddered. He sucked on his lips. Sweet notes run through with the tang of salt. Fear tasted fine.

"Don't you like that? Answer me, Jenny. I don't like to be ignored."

She shook her head.

He licked her neck again. "Don't you like it, really? Doesn't it turn you on? Say it, Jenny. I want to hear the words."

"No." Her voice so small you could hold it in one hand and have room for two more. "No, I don't like it."

"You liked it earlier." He murmured the words as he nuzzled around her ear. "You liked it a lot."

She tried to pull away from him but he held her tight, squeezing just that little bit harder so that the pain showed in her face. He liked how what he did to her registered so easily. It gave him a kick.

"It's been a pleasure working with you."

"Why me?" The tight words extruded through her lips.

He laughed. "It wasn't you, Jenny. It was never about you."

"Then why…"

The bewilderment on her face was a joy to behold. Michael took a moment to anticipate the pleasure of wiping it off.

"It's about Charlie, Jenny. It's all about your dear, old dad."

She worked her mouth but nothing came out. She'd thought she was it with her tight little ass and her high pony tail swinging, but she was nothing. He'd built her up, turned her into a goddess, now he was going to enjoy tearing her apart with a few incisive words.

"We needed to get to him, you were the shortest route. The fact is, Jenny, you just don't matter that much."

"But I don't understand."

Her voice had all the energy of a wilted rose petal.

"It's not that difficult, Jenny. I thought you university students were supposed to be clued-in. No? Okay, I can see by your face that I'm going to have to draw you a picture. You paying attention?"

A laugh rattled in his throat when she nodded.

"Your dad took something that didn't belong to him. The man he took it from, he wants the something back. Simple as that. You're just the insurance to make sure Charlie coughs up. You want to know how we got to him, do you want to see what daddy saw?"

He looked deep into her eyes, wanting to be completely in the moment when she got it, when she finally understood. He was rewarded by a tic, a twitch, a flicker of the eyelid.

"No." The word a whisper of a whisper.

Michael smiled. "I'm going to let go now. I don't want you to do anything stupid, Jenny, okay? Do nothing but stand there."

He released his grasp on her wrists and took his phone from his pocket. She stood motionless, stricken like a bird with a broken wing as Michael flicked through the images.

"Look, that's a good one, very clear. Lots of detail. One for the family album, eh?"

Jenny closed her eyes, "No."

He grasped her face and held the screen in front of her.

"Open your eyes, Jenny. I want you to see what he saw. Do you think he'll be proud of his little girl?"

For a moment he thought she would cry. He could see the tears brimming, threatening to spill, but just as they were on the brink of tumbling over the rims of her eyes and flowing down her pale cheeks, they subsided. She swung her dry gaze to meet his and gave him a look of sheer hatred.

Michael laughed.

"C'mon, Jenny. You've got a date with daddy. He can tell you himself what he thinks."

Chapter 43

Michael snuggled against her as they left the flat. A loving partner, walking with his arm around her. At least that's what it may have looked like to the casual observer. A more attentive looker-on may have noticed that his hand gripped rather than held her arm, and they may have wondered what his hidden hand was doing behind her back.

She knew, Jenny knew.

His hidden hand had snuck up beneath her top. In this hand he held a knife, the blade of which lay flat against the bare skin of Jenny's lower back. He whispered instructions in her ear and used the threat of cold metal and his hard grip to guide her.

"Press it."

The words mumbled in her ear. His hot breath like acid on her skin. He squeezed her arm just a little tighter. Jenny pressed the lift call button. From a distance came the soft clicking and whirring of gears set in motion. A muffled *ting*, and the doors opened.

Michael nudged her forward. She complied with the enthusiasm of a lamb entering a slaughter house. He pressed the blade harder against her skin. Jenny's reflection scowled back at her as she stepped into the lift. Even with the flattering combination of smoked glass and soft light she looked rough. Her face puffy and bruised. Her hair mussed up and tangled. Michael looked rougher still, his eye ugly and swollen, the vicious cut trailing his cheek.

A sick smile appeared on his face when he saw her looking. She dropped her gaze. He was a monster, a psychopath. She should have run the pizza slicer across his throat.

She told herself she would kill him if she got the chance, but the words ran hollow in her mind. She hadn't even been able to hit him when the opportunity had been presented on a platter. But that was because of his eye. The oozing repulsed her and the horror of the damage she had wreaked had taken her by surprise. Next time, she argued, next time she would not hesitate. *Please let there be a next time.*

Michael pressed against her as he leaned forward to push the button for the carpark. She thought about biting his face, of ripping a chunk right out of him, but he held the blade hard against her. Depending on the way he flexed, it could slice straight into her right kidney. *Do it, do it anyway.*

A hand appeared on the door.

"Hold please."

The hand was followed by a body. A hipster type. Large of beard, small of jacket, tight of jean. He skipped into the lift, his thanks freezing on his lips as he caught sight of them. He looked like he wanted to skip right back out again but the doors were already closing behind him.

"Whoa, you guys okay?"

"Been in a car crash." Michael jabbed the point of the knife into Jenny's back as he spoke.

"Looks nasty."

"You called that right." Michael had all the answers.

The hipster was standing as far away from them as he could in the confined space. Jenny tried to catch his gaze, but the guy was looking everywhere but her face, He *knew* something was up, he *knew* the scene was all wrong but he was not for getting involved. Even so, if she reached out to him…

Perhaps he sensed what was in her mind, or perhaps she gave herself away with the tiniest of movements. Whatever way it broke down, Michael increased the pressure on the knife as he turned the blade a degree or two. She tensed as the tip of the blade stung her flesh.

"You okay, sweetheart?"

His voice trickled into her ear as blood trickled from the wound he had made in her back. He ensured his whisper was just loud enough to be heard by the hapless witness as he increased the pressure on the knife. "It will be fine, you'll see."

She nodded, willing him to stop. She told herself that she

would be okay, but as the metal nicked at her skin her faith in the words evaporated.

There was a *ting* as the lift stopped at the ground floor. Michael tightened his grip on her arm. The doors opened. The bearded one bolted like a rat out of a trap, giving them – her – not so much as a backward glance. Anger bubbled and boiled within Jenny as the doors closed behind him. He knew, *he knew* – he should have done something. But he didn't want to see, didn't want to know. He didn't want to get involved.

If it had been the other way around she would have done something. *Really? Would she?*

Jenny's eyes stung and her throat constricted as the lift carried them down to the carpark. *She had to do something.*

When the doors opened again she made a break for it. He thought she was a done deal and so she caught him by surprise. A kick on the shin, an elbow in the gut, followed by a sharp exit.

His hand snatched behind her, catching a few strands of hair. It screamed from her scalp, tearing skin, but she did not stop. Not now. She ran. Her feet pounding on the concrete floor, his thudding behind.

She ran between rows of polished cars and empty bays, seeking the exit – or someone who could help. Someone who could stop him. She spotted the ramp to the street and belted towards it. When she got to the street she would scream. Run into the traffic. Holler at the top of her voice. Someone would hear. Someone would raise the alarm.

She was at the bottom of the ramp when the world turned upside down. A kick to her ankle sending her feet all wrong. She let go of her bag and caught a glimpse of the outside world as she tumbled and span. Walls, ceiling, cars, barely landing on the unyielding floor before he hauled her up, grabbing her by her hair, her clothes, her arms. Waving the knife in her face, screaming at her. She saw blood. Didn't know if it was his or hers. And then he was stuffing her into his car. Forcing her head down, pushing her in. The door slammed. She tried to open it, but he locked it on her. He ran to pick up her bag and threw it in the car. Then he was in the car, in her face, his features hard and twisted, right up against hers, the knife so close to her eyes it was out of focus. She could feel the heat radiating from him as he roared in her face about the mess she'd made of his upholstery. Calling her a dirty bleeding bitch. It was so absurd she almost laughed. She should be feeling fear. The blood was apparently hers and so she should be feeling pain, but she was numb inside.

His bout of bad temper ceased abruptly. He put the knife in his pocket and sat back in his seat. He stared straight ahead for a moment before starting the car. When he spoke as they pulled out of the bay his words were calm as the eye of a storm.

"If you try anything like that again, I will cut your throat and let you bleed out."

Now she felt the fear so strong she could taste it.

Chapter 44

Friel called Boyle and told him where exactly to bring the gear. He'd just hung up when Bobby Big Cheeks arrived. Friel back in his chair and regarded him. Bobby stared back through big soulful eyes set in an acreage of face. Bobby talked. It didn't take long to relay what he had to say. Bobby was not a waster of words. A smile snaked across Friel's lips as he contemplated the news. This was one messenger he would not be shooting.

The news was good. The interlopers had received the message loud and clear and had cleared off. At least the ones who still had the use of their knees had gone. The rest were crawling in the gutter. Writhing back to the hinterlands where they would spread the word. Lenny Friel was not to be messed with.

His reputation was on its way to being restored, but this was just the first instalment. Friel would take care of all business tonight. He had no intention of letting his empire crumble. He was giving nothing away and nobody was going to take a thing from him. When news of Boyle's fate pulsed through the back courts, no one would be in any doubt. Lenny Friel was the A-number one top dog in these here parts and that was just how it was going to stay.

He was on a roll. He could feel it in the marrow of his bones. Everything was going his way. The world was back on its axis and Lenny Friel was calling all the shots. He made the decision there and then, when he'd sorted out the Boyle business, he was going to sort out the situation on the home front. It was time Debs and his daughter got back into line. They needed to show some appreciation. They needed to show respect.

Chapter 45

They drove along the dark, deserted streets of the industrial Badlands. It was a landscape of brick walls, chain link fences, barbed wire, steel shutters and the kind of graffiti feted by no-one. Fear gnawed Jenny's gut like a hungry rat. The beautiful numb had worn off. She was feeling everything. The back of her head pulsed where hair had been ripped from her scalp. The knife pricks in her back stung and sang. There were bruises. Where? Everywhere. But the fear didn't come from what had been done. The fear was in the unknown. It was in the thought of what might come next.

Her mind felt small and confined. She realised she was not thinking properly. Not thinking coherently. Even so, she could not imagine any version of the story she was trapped in ending well. Her only hope was to reach out to Michael. To somehow connect with any humanity within him, if it existed at all.

"I cared for you."

Four words, voice low, barely a sound at all, and yet he heard them. She could tell by the way the corner of his mouth twitched.

"Did you feel anything for me at all, Michael?"

He laughed. If milk made a noise when it curdled, this would be it.

"I know what you're doing."

A response was good. It hinted of a barrier coming down.

"I'm trying to understand, Michael."

"Then understand this, *Jenny*." He sneered her name. "You can try to build a relationship with me, to get me to see you as a person – that is what you're doing, right? See it in a movie did you?"

He glanced at her, grinning. Jenny winced as fear took a chunk right out of her.

"Try if you will but it won't get you anywhere. It won't change a thing. You see, *Jenny Boyle*, your little life means nothing to me."

"I don't believe you." Her voice as faint as a ghost at dawn.

Michael laughed again and shook his head. "The first man I killed was my father."

Images in Jenny's head of a man slipping from a platform, landing in front of a train. A flash of orange, streaked with red. People screaming.

"You said it was an accident."

"I said he didn't kill himself. And he didn't slip. He was pushed. I pushed him."

He said it as though it was nothing. "No…"

"But yes, Jenny, yes."

"Why?" The word barely there. She didn't want to know, not really. Not at all. But some communication was better than none. Wasn't it…

"I was sick of his whinging. I was sick of his self-pity. All I did was put him out of his misery. I suppose it was a personal kill. The others were pure business. You should see the look on your face right now, Jenny. Those ones died slow. I watched the life seep right out of them. I saw their eyes grow dull. But you know, I've never killed a woman. Not yet."

"You're a monster. I can't believe I ever fell for you."

"Don't sweat it. You're not the first and I doubt you'll be the last, though it's going to be harder now, with the mess you made of my face."

Jenny sank back into her seat as a dark silence emanating from Michael filled the car. And when he spoke again, fear swallowed her whole.

"You'll pay for that."

Chapter 46

There came the screech and rumble of the yard gate being rolled back. Friel glanced at Bobby. Bobby walked to the window and peered through the blind.

"Killian."

"Has he got the girl."

"Aye." Bobby nodded.

There was a clatter as the pair climbed the few stairs to the office door and then it opened and there they were. Friel allowed himself a moment to take in the scene. They looked like a pair of refugees from a war zone. She was all banged up and Michael had half his face missing.

"Problem?" Friel asked.

"No." Killian scowled.

Friel snorted. "Looks like this wee lassie got the better of you."

Killian's eyes flashed as Bobby sniggered. He pushed the girl into the middle of the room and reared up at Bobby. "What are you laughing at?"

"I'm laughing at a right clown, son."

Friel watched the pair of them. They were like a couple of weans winding each other up. He wondered what would happen if he unleashed them for a square go. Some dog fight it would be. They'd go at it until the death. People would pay good money to see such a spectacle. There might be something in that. Friel stored the idea away for later.

"Settle down boys, we've got a guest." He turned his attention to the girl. "Your da's been a bad boy."

She looked like she was ready to fall apart, but fair play, she jutted out her wee jaw and had a go at him.

"He's got nothing to do with me and I've got nothing to do with him."

Friel shook his head. "I see where you're coming from and all that, but it's tough titty. You see this is a case of the sins of the father being visited on the daughter and your father has been sinful in the extreme."

Chapter 47

Boyle watched as a red Audi 5 rolled into the breakers yard. The guy on gate opening duty was about as ugly as it was possible to get and still be legal. He closed the gate behind the Audi and slunk back into the shadows. Best place for him. Not even a mother could love a face like that.

The car door opened and a male got out. Boyle couldn't see his face but from the way he held himself he looked young and fit. The light caught his mug as he scooted around to the passenger door. Looked like someone had given him a good doing. He opened the door and pulled someone from the car. Boyle didn't need a spotlight on her to recognise Jenny.

His fingers curled, atoms of rage exploding from his useless fists as Jenny was dragged and hauled to the yard office. He knew straight away that the one doing the dragging and hauling had been on the other end of the lens. The images flashed into his mind once more, blinding him to all reason. He wanted to explode from the car and tear that place apart. He wanted to gouge eyes and rip heads from necks. He wanted to stomp them into inexistence.

While it lasted, his wrath was all consuming. When it subsided, Boyle knew he had to get a grip. He was no use to Jenny if he was blind with anger. Jenny had to be his focus. Jenny. Not the photographs. Jenny.

One goon on the gate. Another in the car. How many in the cabin? Neither of those two was Friel, he was sure of that, so at least one other. Probably more. He'd find out soon enough.

Boyle switched on the engine, put the car into gear and drove up to the gates. He flashed the lights and watched as the gate keeper slunk out from the shadows. Up close, he didn't look anywhere near as handsome. He was like something out of Grimm's Fairy Tales, with the emphasis on grim. The gate keeper gazed at him through hooded eyes, dragging the moment out longer than necessary before rolling the big gate aside.

Boyle put the car into gear and drove into the yard. His spleen twitched as the gate was rolled closed behind him.

Chapter 48

Killian wore a cool visage as Friel postured in front of Jenny. Well as cool a visage as he could muster considering his eyeball was mush and had swollen up like a pensioner's leg on a long haul flight. Inside, he seethed. First chance he got, he was going to take Bobby Big Cheeks down.

The fat-faced bastard was just for starters. Friel was the main course. Who the hell did he think he was, humiliating him like that in front of *her*. Killian's blood bubbled and boiled in his veins as he thought about it.

Friel thought he was top dog, well every dog had their day and Killian's day was about to dawn. He didn't give a flying fuck about this Boyle character. If anything, Boyle had done him a favour, weakening Friel's grip as he had. But his bitch daughter was getting it. No way was she getting away with blinding him. Which meant he'd have to take care of Boyle as well. One more wouldn't make any difference.

That left a question mark hanging over Spanish Tony. He was a weirdy and no mistake. He'd been hanging around Friel like flies round shite ever since Killian had been on the scene, but Killian wondered just how loyal Quasimodo was. Friel certainly never did him any favours. Spanish Tony was just always there in the background, like a manky old mutt everyone had long since given up petting.

Killian had no strong feelings either way. If the mutt got in the way, he'd be dealt with along with the rest of them. And if he didn't get in the way, well maybe a touch of kindness from Killian would go a long way towards buying his loyalty.

He felt much calmer now that he'd decided to kill them. All he had to do now was figure how it was going down.

Chapter 49

The man behind the desk was in charge. He had cold eyes. Like a snake. Michael may have hidden his true self from her but she could feel his hostility towards his boss. But the cold-eyed boss didn't know it. He was so puffed up with his own self-importance he couldn't feel Michael's loathing.

The other one was big and scary looking, but he had sad eyes, like a hound dog. He put them to use looking her up and down. She wondered if he'd seen those photographs. The thought made her feel sick, but weird though it was, Jenny felt safer in the company of the three men than she did with Michael alone.

Michael alone would slit her throat without much provocation. Another dynamic was in play here, one which kept him in check. She was surrounded by monsters for sure, and the tension in the room was palpable, but if she kept her wits about her perhaps there was another way for the story to end after all. The key was staying sharp, watching for an opportunity. No more panic. No more fear. If she let it engulf her again she was done.

She had seen all of their faces and had an idea of where this place was. Michael didn't even try to hide where he was taking her. They were going to kill her. In their eyes she was already dead. They had used her and written her off. Accepting that gave her an edge, just as long as she was willing to do whatever it took to prevent them.

Kill or be killed. Those four words had a calming effect.

The calm lasted for a second. Maybe two. Jenny turned as the door opened. The strange looking man who had opened the gate walked in. Behind him was her father.

Chapter 50

"Jenny."

The gate keeper held Boyle back as he tried to get to his daughter. She had a strange look in her eyes. Like she'd switched off. What had the bastards done to her? He told himself to stay cool.

"Well, well, well, is this him? Is this the famous Charlie Boyle?"

Boyle turned his attention to the man sitting behind the desk. He was all puffed up, sitting on a fancy leather chair. Boyle had seen plenty like it in plenty of offices when he'd been on the job. It was a statement chair, and the statement it made was *look how important I am.*

Boyle looked. Yeah, this guy was important. He was king of the shit-heap. A gallus back-street wide-boy made good. He was also the voice on the other end of the phone. This was Lenny Friel. *Stay cool Charlie, stay cool.*

"Who are you?"

The wide-boy narrowed his eyes. Boyle guessed he wasn't used to being asked who he was.

"The name's Lenny Friel."

"Never heard of you."

Friel looked at the moon-faced heavy leaning against the wall and laughed. The heavy joined in. It was all for show. Behind Friel's narrowed eyes, Boyle could see the wires in his head flaming and shorting-out. He thought he was a big-shot. In reality he was nothing but a drug-peddling loan-shark who'd watched The Godfather too many times.

All he did was exploit his own kind. He was exactly the kind of sleaze sack that made Boyle want to join the police in the first place. Looking at this piece of filth was like looking into the mirror of his past.

While the false laughter rumbled on, Boyle treated himself to a sidewise look around the room. Lenny Friel sat behind the fancy desk in his big pissing-contest chair all dressed up in a fancy suit. Well a sack of shit in a fancy suit was still a sack of shit. Beside Jenny, the Friel-wannabe with the messed up face. The wannabe wasn't for laughing. Against the wall, the snickering moon-faced heavy with puppy dog eyes. And in the middle of them all, Jenny with her vacant face.

Boyle wondered how he'd managed to drift so far from his ideals.

Friel acted like he was the boss of everything, but something wasn't sitting right with this trio. Though he could not read it, Boyle could see that beneath the surface an alternative narrative was running. He glanced over his shoulder at his buddy, the gate-keeper. This guy had something else going on. He was quiet, looking and acting like a dumb lackey, but the troll-faced one was a watcher. Dismissed by the other three, this guy was taking it all in.

"Is that for me?"

Friel was staring at the holdall. Boyle tossed it onto the desk. It skited across the polished surface giving him some pleasure as it trailed a few ugly scratch marks into the varnish. Friel's eyes narrowed so tight it was a wonder he could see anything, but his face adopted a different expression as he stood up and unzipped the bag. He put in his hand and pulled out a plum of a necklace.

"Nice. Very nice." He dug out a few more pieces and held them up. The diamonds danced in the light. Friel was on the verge of purring as he admired them. He looked at Boyle. "We'll consider Sammy's debt paid." He nodded at the wannabe. "Give the man his daughter."

The wannabe pushed Jenny towards Boyle. She stumbled, Boyle caught her and embraced her, hugging her close. "Are you okay?"

She stiffened in his arms and was quick to pull away. Boyle swallowed the rejection. He had a lot of making up to do, but that was for later. If there was a later.

"Happy families, eh?" Friel grinned at him. A diamond bracelet dripped between his fingers.

There was blood in Boyle's eye as he stared back.

"What's the problem, Charlie? Our business here is done. So why don't you take your wee porn star and toddle along."

Boyle had an urge to rip Friel's head off, but the invitation to leave caught him by surprise. He wasn't going to wait to be asked twice. He took Jenny by the arm and, ignoring her attempts to shrug him off, steered her towards the door.

The wannabe stood in front of them blocking the way.

"Michael." A warning shot from Friel.

The wannabe glared at them with his good eye but stepped aside. That was two names Boyle knew now. It didn't feel healthy, didn't feel right, but there was the door right in front of them.

Boyle was staring into the eyes of the gate keeper when Friel piped up again.

"Charlie, before you go."

The gate keeper raised an eyebrow. Boyle nodded. This was it. He turned around. Friel was sitting back in his chair, grinning at him.

"I almost forgot, Charlie. You've paid Sammy's debt, but you haven't paid your own."

"Mine? You've got Sammy's half, you've got my half. That's all there is."

Friel gave a humourless laugh and shook his head. "It's not quite as simple as that, Charlie. You see I lost a lot of face over this business, and I can't have that. You're a man of the world - you understand - a man like me lives and dies by his reputation. Don't take it personally, it's purely business, but there is a debt, and it needs paying."

"I don't have anything else."

"Don't be so modest, Charlie. There's you, and there's the lovely Jenny. Tell you what, it's getting stuffy in here. Let's get some fresh air."

Chapter 51

Killian's eye screamed blue murder. There had been no pain killers in the flat. The building was one of Friel's semi-legit developments, used for money laundering. The apartment was a show-flat. It was all front, kitted out to impress prospective buyers, with nothing going on behind the scenes. Pizza and champagne aside, the cupboards were Mother Hubbard bare.

The first aid box fixed to the wall in Friel's office was a torment to him. It surely contained a tub of aspirin, though the way the wound shrieked and wailed, aspirin might not be up to the job. A dose of morphine was more like it. But right now, he'd gladly cut Friel's heart out for a couple of over the counters.

Pain or no pain, there was still pleasure to be had from the look on Boyle's face when he turned around. The man must have known he was never going to be giving it auf wiedersehen as he walked out of the door, but Friel had given him hope. Nice touch.

"Cable ties," Friel told Spanish Tony.

Boyle resisted when Spanish Tony pulled his arms behind his back, but the resistance was quashed when Friel offered Boyle a live re-run of the photographs. Pain almost overridden, Killian watched Boyle with interest, thinking that if spontaneous combustion was actually a thing, Boyle might just go up in flames right in front of them.

"And her."

Killian stepped forward at Friel's order.

"Not you, him." Friel indicated Bobby Big Cheeks. "Don't want to risk the lassie hurting you again, Michael."

Bobby smirked as he brushed by Killian.

Michael Killian had hated and snarked on people all his life, but humiliated by Friel he now found new, unplumbed depths to his capability for sheer and utter loathing. He had killed the man who fathered him and lost no sleep over doing so. Killing his surrogate would be more difficult but infinitely more pleasurable.

Once Boyle and the girl had their wrists cable-tied behind them, the entire ensemble trooped out to the yard. Spanish Tony drove Boyle ahead of him like a lion tamer wrangling an uncooperative beast. Bobby strong-armed the girl with little grace. Friel played the ringmaster, strutting behind them, whilst he, Michael Killian, was the clown bringing up the rear.

Friel brought them to a halt in front of the baler. Spanish Tony had pre-loaded a car for the demonstration. Friel wanted Boyle and the girl to fully understand what lay in store for them.

He ordered Killian to start the machine. That was Spanish Tony's job, but Killian swallowed it and did as he was told. He'd have his moment and Friel would get what was coming soon enough. He fired the machine up, picturing Friel inside the Peugeot, doors locked, hands banging against the windows as the baler lid came down.

As the baler crushed down the car, Friel delivered a spiel about how efficient it was, his voice riding over the grind and crunch of metal. He had it all planned out. This moment was going to put the seal on Friel's reputation, and he was loving every minute of it.

Bobby Big Cheeks was lapping it up. Thought he was right up there with Friel. Well Killian had a thought or two about that. He barely spared a glance for Spanish Tony. There was nothing new to see in his ugly mug. Boyle's face was etched in hard lines, his mouth a grim stroke of the pen. Maybe he should let Boyle loose on Friel, keep his own hands clean. It was a thought. The girl had closed her eyes but was otherwise keeping it together. Killian admired that, but he was going to kill the bitch all the same. A life for an eye.

He wished it would stop throbbing. Felt like it was pulsing right out of his face.

Friel launched into his second act. He thought he had the world in order. His order.

"Here's how it's going to play out, Charlie. You and your lassie are going to get into your car and you're going to take a wee spin. Think of it as a bonding experience. A chance to make amends before you meet your maker. It'll not take long. You've seen how quick and efficient it is, and then everything will be tied up nice and neat. Know what I mean?"

"NO!" The girl screamed like she'd finally woken up to what was going on. Her outburst caught Bobby by surprise. Killian snorted as she momentarily wriggled free of Big Cheeks' grasp.

Boyle lunged for her, but Spanish Tony kept a grip of him.

Friel frowned at the carry on. "Shut her up, I can't hear myself think."

He'd be pissed off that his big moment had been disrupted. In a small and petty way this amused Killian.

The girl yelped as the thug yanked back on her arms before leaning in and putting a finger on her lips. "Shut the fuck up." The words delivered straight into her face.

Now it was Boyle's turn to pipe up. "You've made your point, Friel. You don't need to do this."

Friel looked back at him, acting like he was actually thinking it over. "Aye, but the thing is, Charlie, I do need to do it. I told you, I lost face because of you."

"You've got the diamonds, the whole haul. You've sent a message out – nobody's going to mess with you."

"I hear you, Charlie. I do, but you know what it's like out there. The diamonds aren't enough."

"At least let Jenny go. She's got nothing to do with this."

Friel adopted an expression of faux concern. "I'd love to help you out, Charlie, I really would, but she knows too much. To be honest, it's all your fault she's involved in the first place."

Friel looked at Jenny. "Sorry love, but if you want to blame anyone, blame your da."

Boyle looked like he'd have chewed Friel's face right off his skull if he'd been within biting distance.

Killian played out the angles as the scene unfolded in front of him wondering how he could turn them to his advantage. If she hadn't done what she'd done to him, Boyle and the girl would have been of no consequence to him. As he couldn't take care of her without taking care of him, that meant the pair of them were dead meat.

Bobby Big Cheeks was going to get what was coming to him while Friel was getting his. Spanish Tony was a grunt. He'd take his orders from whoever was in charge. No threat there. Timing was the key.

Everything was going to move fast once Boyle and the girl were cubed. The baled car would have to be stacked in amongst all the other baled cars. The flat would have to be cleaned up. It would be go, go, go, which meant that perhaps the time for him to make his move was now, now, now.

Why not bring Friel down in front of Boyle, the man who had caused him so much angst. That would add a certain piquancy to the proceedings, no?

Yes, Killian thought. Yes. Time to rattle Lenny Friel's cage.

"Lenny?"

Friel looked at him, clearly irritated by the interruption. "What?"

"How's Debs?"

The look on Friel's face was to die for. He didn't know what the hell was going on.

"She's fine."

"You see much of her lately?"

He enjoyed watching Friel's irritation levels cranking up a couple of notches. "Can you not see, we're a bit busy here?"

Killian shrugged. "It's just that I heard Debs was pretty busy as well these days."

"What are you on about, Michael?" Now he had Friel on the hook.

"I hear she's got… let me see, how to put it delicately? Other interests. That's it. She's got other interests."

Killian glanced at Bobby Big Cheeks. It was a deliberate move, designed to stir up suspicion where none had been before. The funny thing was, when Killian looked at Bobby, he saw displayed upon his vast countenance, the look of someone who had been caught with their hand in the till.

A laugh shimmied through him. Killian's intention had been to spread discord, but in his attempt to knock Friel off-balance, he had inadvertently stumbled upon a delicious truth.

Chapter 52

As soon as Bobby started denying it, Friel knew it was true. Bobby was banging his wife. Friel stared at the baw-heided bastard. He didn't know what hacked him off more – the fact that Debs had played away at all, or the fact that she'd done it with this moon-faced muppet.

He looked at Michael. The one-eyed bastard was pissing himself. He'd deal with him later. He looked at Spanish Tony.

"Did you know?"

Spanish Tony turned his mouth down and shrugged. "Everybody knew, boss."

"They're lying," Bobby blustered. "Both of them, liars. I didn't-"

"Shut it you," Friel snarled. "How did you no tell me?" he asked Tony.

"No my wife. No my business."

Friel wanted to belt him one. Even as he had the thought he realised that's why no-one had told him. They all knew he was liable to rip out the throat of anyone who said anything about Debs. Even if it was true. It was all clear to him now. All the times he couldn't reach Bobby on the phone, and Debs just so happened to be out with the girls. It was true alright.

He turned to Michael. The boy couldn't keep his face straight. Friel would deal with him later, but for now he needed him.

"Get her and tie her to something. Same with you," he looked at Spanish Tony. "Tie him to something and make sure he's secure."

They got busy using cable ties to attach Boyle and the girl to the door handles of a Vauxhall waiting to be scrapped. Meanwhile, Bobby hung about like a wet weekend in Saltcoats. Friel felt sick to the stomach just looking at him.

When Boyle and the girl were secure, Friel went face-to-face with Bobby.

"Tell me, did you do it in my bed."

Bobby spluttered and stuttered.

"If you had the balls to bang her, you should have the balls to own up to it. Tell me, Bobby – did you bang my wife in our marital bed?"

Bobby shook his head. "No, it wasn't like that, it-"

"What was it like then, Bobby? Was it true love?"

"No boss, it was –" he turned his head around as he flailed for the words, looking every inch the drowning man.

"I've had enough," Friel said. "Get in the car."

He watched as the meaning of his words sunk into Bobby's head. Bobby looked at Boyle's car and back at Friel.

"No, you can't mean it?"

"Aye, Bobby, I do mean it. Now get in the car."

Bobby Big Cheeks was Friel's oldest pal, but as Bobby stood in front of him whimpering and shaking, all Friel felt was disgust. "Right you pair, put him in the car."

Bobby ran, but he was slow off the mark and hadn't gone but three strides before Michael and Spanish Tony took him down. He wailed and flailed as they bundled him to his feet and frog marched him to the car where Friel stood waiting.

Any residual feelings Friel may have had for his treacherous former friend were wiped out by the stream of self-pitying tears tumbling from Bobby's eyes and the miserable river of snot flowing from his nose. Friel was disgusted. Bobby had killed men. He had taken lives. Now it was his turn. Live by the sword and all that. This was the game they played. The least he could do at the end of his own was show a little dignity.

He shook his head. "What did she ever see in you?"

"Please, no," Bobby struggled against his captors as he pleaded with Friel. "Lenny, it's me, Bobby, your pal. Remember, you've got to remember. We're pals, you and me, pals. You can't do this, Lenny... Lenny?"

He was an embarrassment.

"Come on man, get a grip," Spanish Tony told him.

Bobby looked at Tony. "Please..."

"You banged the man's wife."

Bobby went quiet. Friel appreciated the emotional depth of the moment, Bobby looking at Tony, Tony looking back at Bobby. This was more like it. There was a quiet dignity instead of all that caterwauling, but as soon as Michael ducked Bobby's head to put him in the car, Bobby started howling again. Friel strode over and slapped Bobby hard across the face. Not a punch, a slap. That was all he deserved for the way he was carrying on. He slapped him again, and again. Bobby shut up. His big, soft eyes filled his head. His mouth hung open, a rope of drool hanging from one corner. At that moment, the only person on the planet Friel was more disgusted by than Bobby, was Debs. How the hell could she have humped this pathetic waste of skin?

"Put him in the car, boys."

Bobby seemed to collapse in on himself as Michael and Tony folded him into the car. Once he was inside he expanded to twice his original size. His big-baw face filled the window, sobbing and yelling and thudding, snot and saliva spattering the glass.

"Sort it."

Spanish Tony climbed into the forklift. Friel glanced at Boyle and the girl, checking that they were watching. Making sure they knew what was coming their way when Bobby had been taken care of. They were watching all right. Backs against the Vauxhall and nowhere to go.

Tony removed the compressed car from the baler and dumped it before spinning the forklift around. Bobby went mental inside the car, squealing and banging on the windows. There was a splurge of red as the forklift prongs drove through the car, but still Bobby bounced and squealed. He was squealing still as the car was loaded into the baler. He kept on squealing right up to the point when Friel pressed the button.

The baler lid descended and the only sound was that of grinding metal.

Chapter 53

Killian watched as the lid bore down on the car. He wondered at what point exactly did Bobby Big Cheeks' life come to an end. How much pain did he feel as the car compressed around him? Standing there watching, it took mere seconds. But time was relative. Time was elastic. Extending excruciatingly for Bobby as bones broke, lungs collapsed, organs turned to slurry, his brain squelching as his skull caved in. It would have been hell in there, seconds stretching to endless hours. Merciful death would have been a long time coming.

Mere seconds though it lasted, no-one would ever be able to say that Bobby Big Cheeks did not suffer at the end.

Friel was all puffed up. Proud of himself for being such a hard man, for being so tough. Diamonds and death, reputation restored to a point higher on the scale than it had previously been. The minus points for his wife shagging around on him more than recouped by the method of Friel's revenge on her lover. Friel was buzzing. Friel was on a high, thinking no-one could touch him. Thinking he was the man.

Killian circled around him. He'd stepped back from centre stage, swimming in the shadows, ever since they'd locked Bobby in the car. Bobby with his big sad eyes. *Boo hoo.* Bobby was gone, God rest his soul, but Lenny Friel was very much alive. For the moment.

Killian looked at Boyle and the girl. They were struggling with the cable ties. Trying to find a way out, but the ties were fastened tight, unyielding plastic slicing deeper into flesh with every tug. They were going nowhere fast. He watched Spanish Tony in the cab of the forklift. He was concentrating on the job, operating levers, doing whatever it was he had to do to make the thing work. Tony was a man of mystery. Could be he had an unfathomable depth of allegiance to Friel. He hadn't wasted any time obeying Friel's orders when it came to wasting Bobby Big Cheeks, but then neither had Killian. Tony was an unknown.

As the forklift removed the cube of metal that contained what remained of Bobby Big Cheeks from the baler, Killian turned his attention back to Friel.

Friel revelled in his moment, his face lit up by the orange flash of the beacon on the forklift. Killian tightened the circle, like a shark closing in on its prey. Lenny Friel could have his moment but the night belonged to Michael Killian.

The forklift deposited the compressed car on a stack of similarly crushed vehicles. Killian fancied he could see a trickle of blood oozing from creased metal. Hard to tell in this landscape of shadows, probably just the romantic in him. He smiled at that as he came to an easy halt at Friel's elbow.

Fascinating how Friel twitched then relaxed as he saw it was Killian hovering nearby.

"Nobody fucks my wife and nobody fucks with me."

He delivered the line with a cold smile. He'd been working on it, now he was trying it out for size. Friel never had been much of a poet. The angels would not weep at his demise. Tony got out of the cab and approached them.

"Good job," Friel told him.

Tony jerked his head. He did not look like a man happy in his work. Interesting. Killian took a long look at Friel, studying the loose gathering of wrinkles in his skin, the way his eyes were hooded by their lids, the course bulge of his nose, the satisfied smile stretching his lips. Aware finally that something was amiss, Friel slowly turned his head and looked at Killian.

"What's the problem, Michael?"

Killian looked at Tony. Tony looked at Killian and then at Friel. His ugly features gave nothing away, certainly no indication that he was ready to leap to Friel's defence. It was when he took a scant step back that Killian knew.

Friel was on his own.

"The problem," Killian told Friel, "is you."

Friel's eyes narrowed. His mouth tightened as he puffed his chest and jutted out his chin. Square go time.

"Come again, Michael."

"You heard me the first time, *Lenny.*"

"Who do you think you are?"

Friel's face was all screwed up as he poked Killian in the chest. Killian stood there and took it, but not for long.

"I know exactly who I am. I'm the guy calling the shots."

Friel sneered a laugh. "You? Have you seen the state of yourself? You couldn't handle that wee lassie."

The muscles on the left side of Killian's mouth twitched. Almost a smile. Friel didn't see the punch coming. Killian felt like his fist was into Friel's soft gut all the way to his wrist. His former boss doubled over. Killian stepped back and gave him time to recover. He wanted to be looking right into Friel's eyes when he delivered the news.

Friel tottered like an old man before straightening up and when he did, there was murder in his eyes. He looked at Spanish Tony. Tony shrugged. "Sorry, boss."

"So it's like that is it?" Friel growled. "Mutiny in the ranks."

"You're a dead man, Lenny," Killian told him. "You and Bobby – you've had your day."

"Now wait a minute, boys." Friel held up his hands. "This has gone far enough."

"No," Killian told him, "we've got a wee bit further to go yet."

He took his knife from his pocket and opened it up.

"Come on..."

Killian looked into Friel's eyes and read his soul. He was amused by how Friel's mind raced in time to the pitter-patter of his heart. The man couldn't believe what was happening. Couldn't understand how the game had been flipped. Friel looked to Spanish Tony for succour.

"Tony, come on, how far back do we go?"

"Almost as far back as you and Bobby."

No comfort to be had there, so he chanced his arm with Killian.

"Michael, I've treated you like a son…"

Friel's eyes were on him, all over him as he played the dad card, begging him, pleading with him. Tasty, tasty, very, very, tasty. Killian's features softened as he gazed upon his surrogate father. It was a nice moment. One to be cherished.

"So you have, Lenny, so you have."

A spark of hope ignited in Friel's eyes. Sucker.

"Remember the accident your old man had in the subway? People were saying he committed suicide – but I supported you all the way, Michael. Your old man would never have done himself in."

Friel brightened as Killian smiled wide and deep.

"You're dead right, Lenny."

"I had your back, Michael. I've always thought of you as the son I never had."

"No, I mean you're dead right about my old man. The useless bastard never would have killed himself. That's why I pushed him."

That put Friel's gas at a peep. Killian was going to give him a moment to let the implications sink in when Spanish Tony muscled in on the scene.

"No room for sentiment in this game, Lenny, that's what you always said."

The man clearly had some kind of a beef with Friel. Maybe having to murder Bobby on Friel's orders had something to do with it. More likely there was a whole other world of resentment and raised hackles running through the decades.

"Aye but…"

Friel spluttered and stammered as Tony produced a switchblade. Tony eyeballed Killian. Killian gave him the nod and the two of them moved in.

"I didn't need him, Lenny, and I don't need you."

"No, no…"

Friel's pleas ended with the first thrust of Killian's knife. He groaned as the blade plunged into him and again as Killian pulled it free. They took it in turns, each stab wound earning a groan weaker than the one which went before. As

Friel leant into him, Killian delivered the final fatal cut with a stab to the heart.

Friel slumped. He lay in the grime, Killian and Spanish Tony standing over him, panting with the exertion of his execution.

Tony toed the body. "No room for sentiment."

Chapter 54

"Stop pulling – you'll only tighten them."

"What do you want me to do dad, just stand here and wait till they come for us? They are animals."

Boyle watched as the two remaining hoodlums repeatedly stabbed Lenny Friel. No argument from him, they were animals, but at least whatever in-fighting was going on had bought them some time. *Where the hell was Elmer?*

"Stay cool," he told Jenny.

"Go to hell, dad."

"That's no way to speak to your father."

Jenny's eyes widened as Elmer emerged from the shadows.

"What kept you?" Boyle asked him.

"I wanted to see how it played out."

"Jesus Christ, it's not a matinee performance."

Elmer looked at the murder scene. "No, but they are very theatrical, these guys. They know how to put on a show."

"Stop your blethering and cut us free."

"Ladies first."

Boyle ground his teeth while Elmer smiled at Jenny as he brandished the wire cutters. She scowled at him in return. He cut her free from the car, then cut the cable ties from her wrists.

"That looks sore."

Jenny scowled some more as she flexed and rubbed at her wrists.

"C'mon, hurry up," Boyle urged. The man had no sense of urgency.

Elmer ambled over and snipped him free. His wrists hurt like hell, the plastic biting through skin into the thin layer of flesh below.

"Uh-oh, trouble." He nudged Elmer.

The murder party had finally woken up to their audience and were bringing the action to them.

The one with the butchered face challenged Elmer. Friel's

blood dripped from the knife in his hand.

"Who the fuck are you?"

"I'm Elmer. Who the fuck are you?"

"His name is Michael Killian," Jenny said. "He's a monster."

Killian laughed as he turned his attention to Boyle. "Did you enjoy the photographs?"

A snarl rode through Boyle, but before he could react, Jenny was on Killian, scratching and clawing like a crazed alley cat. Boyle grabbed a hold of Killian's knife arm before he could do any damage while Elmer dragged Jenny from him.

"I'm going to kill you," Boyle growled at Killian.

"Come ahead."

Boyle eyed the dripping blade. "It's easy to be the big man with a knife in your hand."

Killian tossed the knife aside. "I'm going to rip your head off, Boyle."

Boyle went for him.

Chapter 55

Jenny struggled to get out of Elmer's grasp. She wanted to get at Killian, she wanted to kill Michael herself. This wasn't her dad's fight – it was hers, and she wasn't going to let him take it away from her.

She screamed at Elmer to let her go. Elmer told her to calm down and he'd think about it. Jenny settled, giving him what he wanted so that she could get her own way.

Spanish Tony was standing nearby, watching Boyle and Killian as they rolled about in the muck, biting and gouging, delivering short punches. For all the emotion expressed on his face, he could have been standing in a supermarket queue.

"Man, that is one ugly brawl," Elmer said.

"True that," Spanish Tony agreed.

Jenny looked at the pair of them. Weirdos and freaks, the world was full of them.

Elmer made a joke about the fight. The other laughed. Elmer relaxed his grip on her for but a second and she was out of it. She darted to where Michael's knife lay and picked it up. Elmer cried no, but Jenny was already in amongst it. Her father and Michael rolled and writhed in the muck. Fifty-fifty. She raised the knife and plunged it down. The blade cut through fabric, sliced through skin and gouged into a major organ. Jenny twisted the blade. Boyle fell away from the fight. He stared at Jenny, shock slapped across his face, but her attention was on Michael.

He gasped as she turned the knife. He stared at the dark stain spreading across his shirt before raising his head.

"I didn't think you had it in you."

He gave one final sardonic laugh before his eyes glazed.

The four of them – Jenny, her father, Elmer and Spanish Tony - stood in a circle, watching as the life seeped out of Michael Killian. When he'd breathed his last, Jenny knelt down beside him and went through his pockets till she found his phone.

"You after the photographs?"

She nodded at the man with the ugly face. Her own felt like a blank mask.

"You'd better get Lenny's as well."

She made a move to go to the other dead body, but her father put his hand on her arm and told her he would get it. She let him. Why not? The whole mess was his mess. Everything that had happened to her - his fault. She watched as he hunched over the corpse like a scavenger picking over remains. He found the phone and brought it to her.

"We'll get rid of them later. Away from here."

Jenny put it in her pocket alongside the other and thought of how much humiliation was contained in one small place.

Her father was staring at the man with the ugly face.

"He's cool," Elmer said.

"Who is he?" her father asked, still staring at the man.

"They call me Spanish Tony."

"Are we done with the killing?" her father asked him.

"There's been enough already."

"You going to let us leave quietly?"

Spanish Tony shrugged. "I don't have any beef with you."

"Nor me you."

"You help me with a little housekeeping and we'll call it square."

Her father nodded. "Stella still on watch?" he asked Elmer.

"Yup."

"Call her and tell her we'll be out soon."

Elmer nodded and made the call. Jenny wondered who Elmer was and who was Stella then realised that she didn't care. She didn't want to know. She only wanted the nightmare to end.

Her father looked at Michael's body.

"Baler?" he asked.

Spanish Tony nodded. "And Lenny. We'll put them in Lenny's car. Not you," he said to Jenny. "There's a bathroom in there the office. Go clean yourself up."

Jenny didn't argue. She'd had enough of dead bodies and car crushers. She fetched her bag from Killian's car. In the bathroom she stared at herself in the mirror above the sink. She looked like Sissy Spacek at the end of Carrie, but the gore and grime ran deeper than her skin. It was going to take more than a splash of water to cleanse her.

Her relationship with Michael had been a lie. Her relationship with her father was a lie. Clear water ran foul as she rinsed her face. Blood and lies. And death.

She had killed a man. Taken a life. A bad man, for sure. A man capable of doing terrible things. But a life was a life and she had taken his.

She wondered how she felt about that.

Chapter 56

"What about the stones, you got any interest there?"

Boyle ached long and ached empty. There was no joy in humping dead bodies around. There was even less joy in having a daughter who hated him. And it was clear that she did hate him. Her loathing of him was writ large in every gesture. His life was a void. And now the gangster with the ugly face and daft name was asking him about the diamonds. It always came back to the diamonds.

Once upon what seemed a long time ago, they had represented freedom and a future of blue skies and warm sun, but the dreams had turned sour. The sky was grey, the wind cold, his life empty.

They used Friel's Range Rover, it was bigger than Killian's Audi, and higher off the ground. Much easier for stowing bodies. They lifted the dead weights, loading Friel in the front and Killian in the back then Spanish Tony got busy with the forklift again. They watched in silence as the baler ate the car.

When blood, bone and metal were as one, Elmer called Stella.

"It's done. All over. I'll come fetch you."

As Elmer ambled off, Spanish Tony asked, "Who is this Stella he keeps calling?"

"She's the reason."

As answers went, this one was living next door to cryptic, but Spanish Tony didn't question it. Instead he came back with a question of his own.

"What about the stones, you got any interest there?"

Boyle had this thing about living on Mexico's Pacific coast. Probably something to do with a movie he had seen once. Plus, Mexico was a cheap place to live. The diamond money would go a long way there. He'd had it all figured out. Trouble was, he'd figured it wrong.

"What stones?"

"You sure?"

"I'm sure." Boyle said.

Spanish Tony nodded. That was it then. They were gone. Out of his life for good this time. They had brought nothing but trouble, now that they were gone perhaps his luck would change. It was nothing more than coincidence that Elmer returned with Stella by his side just as Boyle was thinking about his luck changing. He got that old familiar flutter inside when he laid eyes on her. Maybe, just maybe…

"That's some reason," Spanish Tony said.

The pair of them watched as she walked up the steps to the office.

"Take Killian's car," Spanish Tony said, his eyes still on Stella. "There's gonna be a big stink about Lenny. Debs will kick up a fuss, but nobody's going to miss Killian for a couple of days. Dump the car before they start looking for it."

"Okay. Just one thing before we go – let's agree not to cross paths again."

"Done."

Elmer went to the office to fetch Stella and Jenny. Stella emerged with her arm around the girl. Elmer put Jenny's bag in the boot and offered to drive.

"Nice wheels."

Boyle told him to get in the back. Stella offered Jenny the passenger seat but she got in the back. She sat small, all crunched up against the door, about as far away from Elmer as it was possible to get. Or maybe it was Boyle she was distancing herself from. The gulf was deep and the gulf was wide.

Stella got into the front passenger seat. He'd assumed her offering Jenny the front seat was an act of kindness, but maybe she wanted to sit in the back herself, to be as far away from Boyle as she could get. Seemed the only person in the car who didn't loathe him was Elmer.

Spanish Tony rolled back the gate. He gave Boyle a nod as he drove out then rolled the gate shut behind him. Looked like he was planning on slotting right into the space Lenny Friel had left.

They were out of the city before Stella broke the silence.

"What about the diamonds."

"Gone," Boyle said. "Everything's gone."

He had nothing left. His bag, containing everything he owned in the world, which admittedly hadn't amounted to much, had been baled along with Bobby Big Cheeks and Marilyn's car. But at least Jenny was safe. He glanced around at her. She was staring out of the window. He wondered what was going on in her head.

"It was all for nothing," Stella said.

"Not nothing – Frank's gone."

"Yes, I suppose there's that."

She was talking to him. Stella was talking to him. That was something. The two of them sitting side-by-side, that wasn't nothing. They were alive, they were together. That mattered. He wanted to tell her, but the words remained unsaid. The time wasn't right. Maybe it never would be.

There came the sound of cracking and splintering. Boyle glanced around again. Jenny, taking the phones apart. She opened the window and dropped out the pieces, one at a time, letting miles pass between them until there was nothing left.

They stopped at the Broxden services and picked up coffee and food to take away. Despite the caffeine, Stella, Jenny and Elmer dozed off as Boyle drove back up the A9. By the time he was at the Drumochter Pass he had to open the window. Stella woke up then.

"Sorry, I needed the air." He closed the window.

"You okay? You want me to drive?"

Was that genuine concern in her voice? He kicked himself for thinking like this, for being so grateful for any crumbs from her table, for any indication that she had feelings for him. That she cared. Probably it was that she simply did not want him to fall asleep at the wheel and kill them all.

"No, I've got it."

"How's Jenny?" Stella stretched around to check. "Still sleeping. That's good. She's been through a lot."

"I know."

"Are you taking her home?"

Boyle nodded.

"She'll need a story for her mother."

"I know. I'm working on it," Boyle said.

"The best lies are closest to the truth."

"Who told you that?"

"You did."

"So I did." He smiled. "It's good."

"What is?"

"Us, talking like this."

"You have a funny definition of good, Charlie."

"Maybe, but I still like it when we talk."

"What are we talking about?" Elmer's voice from the back.

Boyle and Stella exchanged a look. She smiled at him. The smile gave him hope that there was something there after all.

"Sorry, did I interrupt a moment?"

"It's okay, Elmer," Stella told him. "Charlie and I were just talking, that's all."

Boyle pulled the car up in front of the house he'd once shared with Jenny and her mother. It looked familiar and alien at the same. He switched off the engine.

"I'll get your bag."

Elmer got out of the car and opened the boot. Boyle turned around to speak to his daughter.

"Are you clear on what you're going to say to her?"

"I'm going to tell her I split up with my boyfriend and I just want a couple of days away from everyone."

"Good... are you okay, Jenny?"

"I'm fine, dad. Just fine."

She gave him a look that would have turned Medusa to stone and got out of the car. She took her bag from Elmer and went up to the house. She let herself in without looking back.

Boyle went to start the car, but Stella put a hand on his arm.

"Wait a minute, Charlie."

He looked at her. Her eyes were green in the dawn light.

"Show him, Elmer."

"Show me what?"

Elmer leaned forward and opened his hand. He was holding a bracelet. The diamonds glittered. Boyle's mind raced. He'd made a clean break with Spanish Tony. Jenny was safe and he wanted her to stay that way. He didn't need another Glasgow gangster breathing down his neck.

"Relax, Charlie." Stella read his face. She smiled at him. Even now, with his stress levels peaking, he wanted her. He needed her. "We only took a few pieces."

"Maybe a hundred thou, worth," Elmer said. "Maybe two. Either way, we barely made a dent in the pile. He won't know the difference."

"And we can still dream, Charlie."

Bare feet, warm sand, surf pounding.

Boyle grinned as he started the car.

"Where to?"

THE END

If you have enjoyed reading Boiling Point,
a short review on Amazon would
be appreciated.

Acknowledgements

For their encouragement, support and feedback, I would like to thank Pete Urpeth from Emergents, Avril Souter from Emergents, Phil Jones, and Allan Guthrie. It would have been a harder road without you. I would also like to thank Cynthia Rogerson at Moniack Mhor for helping me get back on my feet when I stumbled. Last but definitely not least, my sincere thanks to you for reading Boiling Point.
Boyle will be back.

www.thrillerswithattitude.co.uk

More by LG Thomson
Available now in paperback and from
Amazon's online Kindle Store

BOYLE'S LAW

"A great read with genuinely heart-stopping moments and cool twists." *****

"An enthralling read." *****

BOYLE'S LAW is a twisting crime thriller set in the heart of the Scottish Highlands. Rippling with dark humour, it's a page-turning read. But with lust, murder and a diamond heist in the picture, be prepared for a view of the Scottish Highlands you won't get on any glossy calendar.

EACH NEW MORN

"Couldn't put it down" *****

"What a cracking read." *****

"An edge of your seat story right from the start." *****

A rogue prion disease has wiped out most of the world's population. Some survivors have been infected by a secondary disease. Aggressive and erratic, they become known as Screamers. They are not the only enemy. Society has broken down. Violent mobs rule the streets. Gangs of raiders swarm through the countryside. Pests and parasites thrive and the worst winter in decades is about to descend.

Who will survive Each New Morn?

EROSION

"What Thomson is best at, is getting inside people's heads and revealing all those thoughts that you and I have all the time about the people around us but don't admit to." *****

"A modern take on classic suspense" *****

Take one remote Scottish island. Add ten people at odds with themselves. Season generously with anger, jealousy and lust. Strap yourself in tight, then sit back and enjoy the ride.

Printed in Great Britain
by Amazon

79513600R00130